PRAISE FC

"From the very beginning, to the last word, this thriller had me hooked and wanting more. A page turner that is an ease to read, vividly detailed and with an ending you wouldn't expect!" ~Brittaney Hubler

• • • • • •

"Wow! What a FANTASTIC read 'Little Lamb' was! Holy smokes!"

After I read 'A flicker in the dark' I thought to myself, there's no way any other book can beat this. Surely I was so wrong! Little Lamb blew it out of the water!

Tom Franks, your first book and you freaking NAILED IT! ~Katie

• • • • • •

"Wow, from the beginning page you are hooked and want to know what will happen next. I am already looking forward to the author's next book! I am eager to have these available to my friends as presents." ~Al Granger

• • • • • •

I love good fiction. This book was a page-turner from the start. No wasted – though some eloquent - words with a riveting ending! ~Ruth Bentler

LITTLE LAMB

To Sharon,

Enjoy the read!

TOM FRANKS

First Edition published by Perfect Publishing, 2022

ISBN: 978-1-64810-123-6

Visit here to communicate with the author:
www.Facebook.com/tomfranksauthor
www.Instagram.com/tomfranksauthor

Printed in the United States of America

For my wife, Brittaney.
Without her love and encouragement,
this book wouldn't have been written.
I love you.

ACKNOWLEDGEMENTS

Duane and Rachael, my parents-in-law, whose support has been unwavering.

My parents, Luci and Mick. Thank you for everything.

Chris and Krissy, friends as well as family, my life has been better with both of you in it.

My younger sister, Poppy, who always inspires me.

Ron and Bianca, thank you for showing me the true meaning of neighbour.

Ken 'Dr. Smiley' Rochon, Jr., PhD, for your confidence, enthusiasm and publishing prowess.

Last, and most certainly not least, Michelle Mras. Without whom, this wouldn't be happening. Thank you for helping me get this opportunity, I will be forever grateful.

PREFACE

Originally a short story I wrote for a GCSE piece when I was sixteen, 'Little Lamb' is the end product of fifteen years worth of patience.

The written word has always been a passion of mine but life got in the way of my own writing. I continued reading, however, and found myself constantly inspired by fantastic authors.

Having been granted the gift of time in late 2020, I was finally able begin the process of writing my own crime-fiction.

My aim with my writing is to create stories that are so gripping, so captivating, that closing the book and putting it down becomes a battle in itself.

I hope you enjoy reading it.

PROLOGUE

November 2019

Staring into the shadows, he sighed and gently closed his car door. The woodland in front of him was pitch black and uninviting and a feeling of unease was growing in the pit of his stomach.

It was raining heavily, the cold air clinging to him in an icy embrace; the road adjacent to the woodland was empty and lonely, the only sound was the hammering of the torrential rain on the tarmac.

He slowly and cautiously walked around his vehicle and took his first step into the woodland. The ground was soft, thick with the decaying bodies of dead leaves and the precipitation had made the footing treacherous and unsteady. He took a second step, a third, a hesitant fourth and he stopped. He stood stationary for a moment and felt the darkness envelope him, the fear so tangible he could taste it. This was it, this was the moment he had wanted for a long time, the moment he had forfeited so much for and the apprehension was crippling.

He forced himself to take another step forward and began his trudge into the woods.

His clothes were heavy with rain water and each shaky, nervous breath drifted out in front of his face and hung there like mountain mist. He was shivering but it wasn't because of the cold – he was terrified. He was terrified, he was alone and he was walking into the unknown.

His heart was pounding so hard, it felt as though it could explode through his chest at any moment; the knot in his stomach was growing with each step he took. He had never felt so trepidatious, so fearful but even though every instinct was telling him to stop, his body was on auto-pilot and was dragging him deeper and deeper into the wilderness.

Following the direction of a dirt track that split the woodland in two, he was careful to stay in the safety of the pine trees and blackthorn. He didn't want to be seen approaching, he wanted the opportunity to adjust to whatever he found – no surprises.

He shoved his way through some of the dense blackthorn, the spines pulling at his clothes like dozens of tiny hands urging him to stop, to turn around, to go back and call for help. He broke through the last part of spiky undergrowth, brushing himself free of any branches that had latched on to his clothing and increased his pace, his shoes sinking into the damp earth, rotting twigs and pine needles crackling beneath him. He couldn't turn back and he couldn't call for help – not yet anyway. He had been disgraced as a detective and no one would listen anymore, he needed something concrete first, something that would make them listen.

His obsession with this case was his downfall, it had taken over his life but he couldn't leave it alone, he couldn't quit. A human life could depend on his stubbornness, on his unrelenting optimism that death hadn't already paid the poor girl a visit. He couldn't write her off like so many others, like his former colleagues – he had to believe she was still alive.

The rain was getting heavier, droplets slamming against the earth in a thunderous crescendo. It was deafening as well as comforting, the din and the battering of the water against his body was an assault on the senses but it reminded him that this was real.

He stopped for a moment and leant against one of the many pine trees. He took some deep, uncomfortable breaths of the damp, frosty air and allowed his heart some time to cease the unrelenting hammering against the inside of his chest. The enormity of this situation was beginning to take hold of him but he had to calm down. Closing his eyes for a moment, he forced himself to relax and try to control his erratic breathing.

After what felt like an eternity, he opened his eyes and something immediately attracted his attention; a small glint of light, reflecting off of a surface in the distance. A vehicle? It was hard to tell but the hopefulness that buoyed his spirit was a wonderful feeling. For a moment, it was like the rain had stopped, like he wasn't completely saturated and petrified. All of a sudden he was moving, it was like an invisible force had shoved him and, once again, he was striding through the woods.

With something to aim for, something to focus on, his pace was brisk, blackthorn and low hanging pine branches ripped at his clothes and tore at the delicate, moist skin on his face, drawing blood. It didn't slow him down, however, he was close. Finally an opportunity to wrap this up was within his reach.

He reached the perimeter of the wood and found himself looking at a 4x4 – the vehicle he had followed here. The source of the glint of light, a house! Two windows, brightness streaming out into a clearing which signified the end of the dirt track and an end to his 'adventure' in the woods. The light glinting off of the vehicle like moonlight shimmering on the surface of the ocean.

He slowly stepped out from the security of the darkness and crouched behind the 4x4, the rain hammering against the exterior of the vehicle sounding like the beating of war drums, heralding the commencement of battle.

Peering up at the house from his position of safety, he drank it all in; a farmhouse, old and in a state of disrepair. A single wooden door and four windows faced forward, a single small window on the side of the building. The old paint peeling off and battling the moss that grew all over. Ivy covered more than half of the old stone work and aged plant pots beneath each window were barren of any life, disconsolate and dingy.

There was artificial light pouring out from two windows – upstairs left and downstairs right. His eyes focussed on the upstairs initially, he could make out old drapes shutting out the rest of the world. He switched his eyes to the downstairs room, no drapes – he could see straight in. He watched for a moment unblinking, waiting for some movement, for a sign of life… nothing.

He turned around and slumped to the wet floor, propping himself up against the vehicle and took a moment to get his bearings. Inside his chest, his heart was thumping away again, the anticipation of what he had to do next making him anxious. He emptied his mind and stood up once again, slowly. He peered into the vehicle, the light from the house aiding his vision. The interior was tidy, immaculate even. Nothing of note as far as he could tell, without risking an attempt at opening one of the doors. It unnerved him, it was too clean.

He tore his eyes away from the vehicle and again focussed on the illuminated downstairs room. He stared for a few moments, unblinking, ensuring there was still no movement before making his approach.

Each step he took was tentative but swift and he never once dropped his gaze from the lit up aperture that was his target. The rain began to ease off as he advanced, the battering of the earth and 4x4 giving way to an eerie silence.

He reached the building and pressed himself against the old stone wall to the right of the window. Somewhere in the depths of the wood, the hoot of an owl reverberated around, a lonely, haunting sound. The strong scent of moss and damp clung to the inside of his nostrils, making him scrunch his nose in disgust.

Warily, he turned his body and peeked through the window. He squinted, his eyes adjusting to the bright light; an old kitchen, dirty and bare, on the hob an old kettle and a few mugs and plates were scattered on the sink draining board, freshly washed. His eyes scanned the room, taking in every minor detail; the clean dishes, the small dining table with two chairs, one of them haphazardly jutting out into the centre of the room.

He looked through the kitchen door, trying to see if there were any signs of life... still nothing. He ducked under the window and approached the front door. The paintwork, once red, was flakey and faded. The brass knob and door knocker were both tarnished, the letterbox only attached on one side. It was clear this place hadn't had any maintenance for a long time.

He reached his hand out toward the knob and hovered near it for a moment, his palm sweaty and his fingers shaking. He grasped the door knob and, for a moment, savoured the cold brass against his skin. He held his breath as he gently turned the knob and gave the door a light push. It crept open with a gentle creak, the musky scent of old wood hitting him immediately. He stood in the doorway, looking into the hallway that was semi-bathed in light from the kitchen.

He took an unsteady step forward and he was in.

CHAPTER 1

October 2016

The shrill beep of his alarm perforated the morning silence for a third time. Detective Sergeant Scott Harris groaned as he rolled over and tapped his phone screen, ending the racket. He had already hit the snooze button twice, a third time wasn't an option – it would make him late. He looked at the time, only six forty-five, and rolled back into his original position. He clenched his eyes shut and roughly rubbed the sleep from them, he *hated* Mondays.

Yawning, he swung his legs out of bed and sat up. He ran his fingers through his thick, dark, unkempt hair and reluctantly got to his feet. Lumbering through to his bathroom to relieve himself, he yawned once more and stretched his arms above his head. Shuffling the last few steps, the need to urinate becoming more urgent, he hurriedly lifted the toilet seat and took aim, the sensation making his body shudder. He flushed the toilet, leaving the seat up and sleepily rotated away to turn the shower on. Having slept unclothed, he was shower ready and he hopped straight in, turning the squeaky tap to trigger the release of the water. He stood stationary underneath the torrent for a few moments, enjoying the warmth of the onrushing liquid, before washing quickly and forcing himself to step back out into the chilly bathroom – no time for a prolonged shower this morning.

He picked up a damp towel from the floor, the only towel, wrapped it around his waist to cover the bottom half of his body and walked over to the bathroom sink. Using one of his large paws, he wiped the steam from the mirror and looked at his reflection. Scott Harris was a handsome man, of Irish descent and he knew he looked good. His eyes were a deep, piercing blue and stood out like two shimmering sapphires against his porcelain skin. A few laughter lines framed the eye socket, softening his features a touch, the frown lines on his forehead having the alternate effect. His hair was jet black and plentiful, naturally tousled; he had no need to style it and it worked for him. He didn't obsess over his appearance, which his unshaven face could attest to, but he tried to stay in shape. He would attend the gym when he could and would jog on weekends, if he had time. He was built big; broad shouldered with large arms and thick, tree trunk legs and at six foot two, he could cut quite the intimidating figure.

He brushed his straight, moderately stained teeth, flossed and then swirled some mouthwash before dropping his towel and walked, nude, back into the bedroom. He wasn't a tidy or organised person, in fact quite the opposite – chaotic would be a more accurate way to describe his living conditions but he couldn't care less. He navigated toward the wardrobe, stepping over and around old clothes that were strewn across the floor. Swinging the wardrobe door open, he yawned again and grabbed some boxers. He pulled them on over his sizeable legs, adjusting himself accordingly and then grabbed a pair of thin, black socks to wear. He sat on the edge of the bed to pull the socks on, then stood up and stretched again. Searching through his wardrobe, he pulled out a smart, blue suit that complimented his impressive physique and a plain, white shirt to go with it – no tie. He got dressed, shirt not buttoned the whole way and stood in front of the mirror, smoothing out his suit with his hands, admiring his speedy handiwork.

He left his bedroom and began his journey downstairs. His house was lovely, decorated immaculately with several pieces of art hanging on the walls, none of which really meant anything to him. The wooden staircase led down to a warm, welcoming hallway that was dominated by an immense, solid oak front door. He walked down the hallway, headed into the kitchen and immediately switched on the coffee machine, which whirred into life. Using one of his large hands like a shovel, he scooped up some empty takeaway boxes and moved them to create space on the kitchen worktop – his version of tidying up. He then delved into the sink to grab an unwashed mug and placed it under the machine, ready to be filled with the dark elixir. Once the mug was brimmed, he opened the french doors which led to the garden and stepped outside.

He shivered before taking a delicate sip of the hot liquid and placed the cup on a small garden table. It was cold out this morning, the English Autumn had well and truly arrived and the weather was getting bleaker by the day – *not* what you want on a Monday morning.

He turned to reach back inside and grabbed a half empty packet of cigarettes from the window sill. Lighting one, he eagerly took a drag and savoured the hit of nicotine. He then stared down at the cigarette that was safely gripped between his index finger and thumb. 'Not the most nutritious breakfast' he said out loud and smiled to himself. Talking to himself in the morning had become a bit of a habit, understandable when he lived alone. This big, beautiful home was wasted on him really; all he used it for was to eat, sleep and defecate.

It had been years since he had a proper relationship, he had the odd fling or one night stand but being a Detective tended to get in the way of a proper personal life. At thirty-eight, he had pretty much given up on the thought of a family and was practically married to his profession and although his own fault, he had grown to resent his job. It asked a lot to be a detective, it took its toll over the years, both mentally and physically. People relied on him to help, relied on him to solve cases and he did! Unfortunately, this wasn't a film and rarely did a case have a completely happy ending. He had lost count of the amount of dead bodies he had seen over the years, lost count of the amount of bereaved family members whose lives had crumbled right before his very eyes. Children, sons, daughters, mothers, fathers; it never got any easier. He had grown a thick skin through his time on the force, almost becoming numb to it all and he wondered whether it was his stunted emotional state that had left him unable to form proper relationships.

He quickly flushed the thought from his mind and tried not to think of his lonely existence – it was too bloody depressing. He took another long drag of his cigarette and closed his eyes, enjoying this brief moment of calm before he had to head to the station. As much as the more serious cases affected him mentally, everything he had recently had been minor, and he missed the challenge – he *craved* the challenge.

Glancing at his watch, he cursed under his breath; seven thirty-five – he should've left five minutes ago! He chugged the remainder of his coffee and headed inside, closing and locking the french doors behind him. Haphazardly blundering around, he hastily gathered up his personal effects, slipped on some smart brown shoes and stumbled out the front door to start his day.

Climbing into his black BMW, he dropped his phone and cursed loudly. He fumbled around under his seat until he located it and placed it safely in the centre console. Pushing the 'start' button, the car roared into life and, with no concern for his neighbours, he put his foot down and rumbled down the street. The drive was only twenty minutes, traffic depending, and he used those precious minutes to clear his head and try and prepare for his day. Pressing play on the touch screen on his dashboard, the melodic sounds of *Queen* filled the vehicle and he sang along heartily to *Under Pressure*. The irony of the title and the nature of his job was not lost on him and he laughed loudly, little did he know, the title of that song would become even more fitting in the coming days.

CHAPTER 2

Staring out of his bedroom window, Michael Thompson allowed himself a small grin. Today was the day, the day he had prepared for for several months. He had been watching her for a considerable amount of time, he was certain she was The One and today was the day they were going to meet. A lot of time and energy had gone into this, he had prepared well. He was exuberant but from the outside you couldn't tell, his demeanour was always very calm and collected, almost nonchalant.

It was still dark outside, five-fifteen on a Monday morning and it was cold. He was already dressed and ready to go; thick socks for warmth covered his narrow, veiny feet, cargo trousers and a T-shirt, both juniper in colour, covered his attenuated, angular frame that didn't suit his six foot one stature. His mousy brown hair was cut short and neatly combed to one side, his beady eyes, usually protected by glasses were today aided by contact lenses – today was not a day for frames. His face was friendly and void of any blemishes, his nose small like a button mushroom and thin lips covered crooked teeth. He looked young for forty-one.

He turned away from the window and began making his bed in the same meticulous method as every morning. All edges tucked neatly, the top edge folded back on itself and the entire surface smoothed out so there wasn't a crease in sight. He took a step back, double-checking his work, before swiftly turning and leaving his bedroom.

His flat was small, just four rooms and a cramped hallway but he made the space work with his scrupulous organisational skills. Walking into the kitchen, he turned on the kettle and patiently waited for the water to boil and, once ready, he made himself a very milky cup of tea. He stood, leaning against the worksurface and tentatively sipped at his tea, worried it may burn his mouth, even with the copious amount of milk he had added. He felt an odd sense of calm, considering the magnitude of the day. Calm was what he did best, however, and today was no time to get the jitters. Finishing his tea, he washed the cup immediately and placed it in the cupboard, neatly alongside the others.

The kitchen was exceptionally clean, in fact, his whole home was spotless; no clutter and everything had a particular place. He hadn't entertained visitors for a long time, when he had it was forced upon him by over-friendly neighbours or overzealous door-to-door salesmen. The thought of having people in his space and his organisation being interfered with made him anxious. It was this nature that made him become very reclusive over the years but the loneliness still crept up on him from time to time. He had often imagined how wonderful it would be to share life with a special someone and now he had found her.

Michael Thompson had no family, he was the product of an incredible mother and an absent father. His mother was a warm, caring person and his bond with her was unique. He was a timid child and she was everything to him, he rarely left her side. It was just the two of them and it was exactly how he liked it but, it turned out, that wasn't enough for her. When he was twelve years old, she took her own life and he lost everything. Thrust into the care system, he was shoved from foster family to foster family; bullied by foster siblings, beaten by two foster fathers, it was a relief when he turned eighteen and could venture out into the world of his own accord.

After ensuring the kitchen was immaculate, he walked out into the hallway and took his coat off the hook. He pulled it on and zipped it up, it was charcoal in colour and waterproof – you can never predict the weather this time of year! He slipped on a pair of walking boots and tied the laces, double knot for security. A woolly hat and pair of leather gloves completed the outfit and he exited his flat.

He glanced at his watch as he walked down the dimly lit outdoor staircase – five forty-five, perfect. Shuddering from the cold, he adjusted his woolly hat so it sat lower, covering his ears completely. Reaching the bottom of the stairs, he glanced around the car park to ensure privacy – it was dead, his only companion the wind, which whistled around him.

He quickly and quietly walked across the car park, the cold wind stinging his cheeks, and approached his vehicle: an old Land Rover Discovery, burgundy in colour. After reaching his vehicle, he took another quick scan of the car park to ensure privacy before opening the boot; it was pristine, not a speck of dust or dirt to be seen. A solitary blanket, neatly rolled up was propped in the corner next to a black holdall. He had a further look around the car park before pulling the holdall forward and unzipping it to expose the contents. Inside, a small roll of blue rope, a roll of duct tape and a first aid kit – everything he needed. He zipped the holdall shut, gently placed it back next to the blanket and closed the boot.

He sauntered around to the driver side of the 4x4 and took his place behind the steering wheel, closing the door quietly behind him. He smiled to himself, this was it! The excitement began to build inside him but he suppressed it, this was no time to relinquish control. He turned the key in the ignition, the car chugging into life and he was on his way.

CHAPTER 3

Sara Williams awoke with a start, the violent sound of her alarm was an unwelcome commencement to her day. She switched the alarm off, rolled over, buried her face into the pillow and moaned.

'This is too fucking early!' she groaned out loud, her volume increasing with each word.

She rolled back over and sat up, pushing her long, blonde hair out of her face and turned on her bedside lamp. She *despised* these early starts but she knew she would never go for a run after work. Throwing her duvet to one side, she swung her legs over the edge of the bed and sat up fully. Grabbing a hair tie off of her bedside table, she roughly scraped her hair back into a ponytail.

Standing up, Sara pulled off the t-shirt she had worn to bed and admired her body in the large mirror hanging on her bedroom wall. She was happy with how she looked, which made these early morning runs worth it. Her figure was of an athletic build and, although only five foot six, her legs were long, muscular and shapely. Her waist was slight, her stomach flat and toned, which worked to accentuate her ample bosom. Her big eyes were a deep jade, her lips full and her teeth brilliant white and perfectly straight. Naturally olive skinned, she had never used a sunbed or fake tan like most of her friends. Her appearance was striking and she gained a lot of attention for it, which she shrugged off with aplomb – looks aren't everything.

Her outfits for the day were prepared the night before, running clothes neatly folded on her chest of drawers and her work attire hung readily on the back of the bedroom door. She pulled on a pair of running leggings and a thermal running top, worn for practicality but it complimented her figure. Finally, she slipped on a pair of ankle socks and a headband to contain any stray hair. She took one last look in the mirror, dressed in all black she looked as though she was wearing activewear for a funeral. She chuckled at the thought and vacated her bedroom.

Flicking on the hallway light, she strolled to the kitchen to grab her water bottle – filled the night before and refrigerated. Her kitchen was beautiful, in fact, her whole apartment was lovely. She had lived here for three months, her first time living away from her parents. Six months prior, she had fallen into a job in sales and excelled quickly, making some considerable commission. This influx of capital afforded her the opportunity to put a decent size deposit on a place and get herself on the property ladder. Her parents, very generously, helped furnish and decorate the place and she felt at home immediately.

She loved the area too, it was quiet and picturesque with adequate parking and a stone's throw away from a lovely, quiet park where she went for her morning jog. She slipped on her running shoes, sighing and rolling her eyes when she saw the mud underneath from her previous run. Placing her bluetooth headphones on, she selected her music, slipped her phone into the snug pocket on her leggings and left the flat with the dulcet sounds of *Bon Iver* ringing in her ears.

Once outside, the cold air hit her with a frosty slap, causing her to gasp from the shock of the cold. She had a brief stretch off and hit the ground running, determined to warm up quickly. The park was only a short distance up the street and she reached the entrance promptly. Fenced on the entrance side, it was surrounded by trees on all other sides; two sides acting as a privacy barrier from other residences and one side had a small woodland. She loved running here in the morning, it was quiet; no other runners or early morning dog walkers to navigate, she could just run. It was well lit along the running path, which surrounded a large grass area, with street lights positioned every twenty metres or so – necessary at six in the morning when the sun was still waking up.

She ran at a brisk pace, relishing the sensation of the cold air on her face. Each stride making a satisfying thud on the pathway. She completed a couple of laps, steadily increasing the tempo each time. She was breathing heavily, steam permeating from her body and her breath leaving a light haze in her wake. She finished her fourth lap and began her fifth and final round.

Although the early morning wake ups were something she detested, the feeling she had when she was on her run was something incomparable to when she tried other forms of exercise. She felt free, she felt in control and it was a short time where she had nothing else on her mind – it was bliss.

Sara upped her speed, as she always did on the last loop and really pushed herself. The lactic acid was building in her legs as she rounded the final bend and she broke into a sprint to finish strong, running adjacent to the woodland. She relaxed and smiled to herself, as she reached the end, and gradually slowed to a halt. She bent down, hands on her thighs, puffing and panting, trying to catch her breath. She stood back up, put her hands behind her head and stretched to open her chest but as she did so, her eyes locked with those of a stranger who had appeared in front of her as if from thin air.

CHAPTER 4

Michael parked his vehicle alongside the entrance to an isolated footpath that cut through a small stretch of woodland. His hands were shaking as he switched off the ignition and turned off the headlights. Nervousness mixed with excitement, apprehension mixed with eagerness, a concoction of feelings and emotions that made this whole moment incredibly overwhelming. Allowing himself a few moments to gain his composure, he took several deep breaths and forced himself to relax. This was a moment that required complete calm and control.

Exiting his vehicle, he once again took a look at his surroundings, he had to remain vigilant – he didn't want any surprises. He left his vehicle unlocked and skulked into the woodland, his shoes scuffing against the soft, damp dirt, crushing the grass as he did so, low lying brambles tugging gently at his trousers. He walked nonchalantly through the trees and undergrowth, not displaying the anticipation that was still building inside him. As he sank deeper into the shadows cast by the large oak trees that loomed over-head, he relaxed increasingly. Michael had spent some considerable time in this patch of woodland early in the morning and was yet to encounter another human being, the large canopy and vegetation concealing him to the point he almost felt invisible.

He arrived at his spot, an area off the path that he had trodden clear across the many visits he had made here. It was a well chosen vantage point with a great view of the whole park and only a few feet away from the pathway. It was still very cold and he hud-dled himself together while he waited and glanced at his watch – almost six o'clock.

Those couple of minutes went by in a flash and she appeared at the entrance to the park. He felt his palms begin to sweat inside his gloves and the familiar flutter in his stomach that happened every time he saw her. She had arrived at six o'clock on the dot, the same as every weekday morning. Oh, how he loved her punctuality.

She had started her run and he watched her intently, his breathing thick and heavy. He felt tense and enlivened, his hands shaking uncontrollably. As she jogged past his vantage point on her initial lap, he sniffed the air hoping to catch her scent but the short distance between them was too great for such treats. It wouldn't be too long before he would be able to close that distance, finally be close to her and the thought made him smirk.

His thoughts quickly turned to the impending execution of his plan and he came crashing down to earth with a painful bump, he hadn't fully decided how to initiate this part. He didn't want to hurt her, he didn't want to harm her in any way. *She passed him a second time.* He had to subdue her until he could get her to a safe place, until he had the opportunity to explain everything to her. He also had to remain undetected, outsiders wouldn't understand! *She passed him a third time.* This first part wasn't going to be easy but he had to have the courage to pull it off – it would all be worth it in the end. The suddenness of these conflicting emotions and the sheer reality of the situation was making him jittery but this was no time for cold feet. *She passed him a fourth time.* Taking a deep breath he forced himself to calm down, suppressing the sudden apprehension.

Focussing on the task at hand, he got back to watching as she ran along the far side of the park. If she stuck to her usual trend, this was her final lap. As she rounded the final corner, she broke into a sprint. His heart was beating so vigorously, it made him feel queasy; the moment he had waited for, the moment he had planned for, was imminent. The thudding of her feet, as she approached at speed, was amplified in the silence of the morning, echoing around the park. He closed his eyes and braced himself… the footsteps stopped, the resonance replaced by the sound of her heavy, gasping breaths.

He opened his eyes and there she was, mere feet away… *so close.* She was bent over, hands just above her knees, trying to catch her breath and he stepped out onto the path. She looked up, bathed in the orange glow of the streetlight and their eyes locked. For a split second he savoured the moment, savoured the connection. His elation, however, was short-lived as he saw her eyes fill with fear. She twitched, as if to run, but he reacted as quick as a cat, drew back his fist and slammed it into the side of her head. The blow was forceful enough to send her sprawling to the ground but not enough to knock her out. Her face was a picture of pure terror as he threw a second punch, this one connecting flush on her jaw, her head rebounding into the concrete with a sickening thud and knocking her unconscious.

He glanced around to ensure the incident had gone undetected before scooping her limp body into his arms; she was light and easy to move, even for someone as feeble as he was. Moving swiftly back into the protection of the undergrowth, he began his journey back to his vehicle with his prize.

As he strode through the small woodland, he began to sob. Although necessary, striking her had upset him beyond words. If only there could have been another way. He looked down into her face, flabbergasted by her beauty and a huge rush of fondness washed over him. She was his now, he had his love in his arms and, despite a turbulent start, he couldn't be happier.

The autumn wind was howling, rustling the fragile leaves that were clinging on to their final moments of life on the outstretched arms of the oak trees. Stomping towards his vehicle with purpose, he knew time was of the essence. He reached his 4x4, awkwardly opened the boot and dumped her in clumsily. He kept looking around, it was nearing full daylight and a disturbance could be catastrophic. He bound her hands and feet with the blue rope, not too tight but enough to keep her restrained and as he placed a piece of duct tape tightly over her lips, she stirred and woke up. This time, there was no hesitation and with a satisfying *thwack*, she was unconscious again. He removed her phone from her pocket, dropped it to the floor and stamped on it repeatedly, smashing it to pieces. He picked up the remnants and put them in his pocket before returning to her.

'Sleep, my little lamb. All will be well soon enough.' he whispered and planted a gentle kiss on her forehead. Concealing her with a blanket, he ensured she was well hidden.

He closed the boot calmly, walked to the driver's door and took his place behind the wheel once again.

'Job done.' he thought to himself as he turned the key in the ignition and drove away.

CHAPTER 5

Marching through the station, DS Scott Harris kept his head down and reached his desk without speaking to anyone. Quietly taking his seat, he looked around, his persistent scowl enough of a deterrent to stop anyone approaching him with any Monday morning niceties.

He scanned his desk, a mess of paperwork – mainly closed cases, some open but nothing too pressing. He shoved it all to one side, trying to create some sort of clear space so he could begin to sort through it all.

Another desk backed onto his, belonging to a young Detective Constable, James Lock. An eager and irritating young chap, who idolised Scott and pestered him like an energetic puppy. Scott could see the youthful DC peering around his computer monitor, cautiously.

'Can I help you, DC Lock?' Scott snarled, not hiding his annoyance at being bothered already.

Lock nervously stuttered his way through a response. 'Just... er... wondered if you, um, wanted a coffee...Sarge?'

The way he asked the question irritated Scott further, this young man was a good detective but his edginess grated on him. Scott stared at him for a few seconds, making James shift uncomfortably in his seat. 'No thank you, James.' The words polite, the tone dismissive and a dejected DC Lock hastily returned to his own work.

Scott Harris has been in the police force for eighteen long years. He became a police officer at the age of twenty and he had cherished his role as a 'Bobby on the beat' in the late nineties. He had been an enthusiastic, young man and his hard work and perseverance had gotten him to his current role in the Criminal Investigation Department.

Scott had worked on some intense cases in his time and earned commendations on multiple occasions. These plaudits had meant something to him back then, they had actually given him a sense of pride at one point. He had grown contemptuous over the years, however, and his love for the job was waning. Scott had invested a lot into his profession over the years, vicariously living every major case that he had worked on. It had drained him mentally and he sacrificed having any sort of real life outside of the job. He had become bitter and resentful and these feelings made him question the job in its entirety. It had made him difficult to work with and, although his success and reputation forced the respect of his peers, his lone wolf persona made his colleagues uncomfortable.

He slipped his suit jacket off, hung it on the back of his chair and began sorting through the mountain of paperwork that was taking up precious real estate on his desk. Colleagues would greet him hesitantly if they walked past and he would meet them with an uninterested, curt nod of the head, never looking up from his desk.

The paperwork vexed him more than anything else. It had steadily increased over the years, decreasing the amount of field work. This royally pissed him off because, to him, this wasn't police work, it was busy work. He didn't understand why they couldn't just employ some paper-pushing twerp to handle it all. He spent a couple of hours begrudgingly finalising the paperwork for the stack of closed cases and then relaxed back into his chair. He gazed down through the desks toward the Superintendent's office and saw that it was empty. 'Perfect.' he thought to himself, he could hand in his paperwork without having to engage in any monotonous small talk with the old toad.

He gathered up the collection of completed files, paced past the other desks into the Superintendent's office and dumped them into his 'in tray' with a satisfying thud. He swiftly spun back around, determined to ensure the avoidance of his superior and headed back to his desk. He had two cases left that he could chase up today, grateful for the opportunity to get out of this hell hole.

'James, I'm gonna head out and look into these.' he barked, holding the two files aloft.

James' eyes widened and he responded eagerly; 'Do you want me to-'

Scott cut him off quickly, 'I'm fine, James.' More disappointment for the Detective.

Scott gathered up his things, grabbed his jacket and left, ignoring the existence of everyone as he did so.

CHAPTER 6

Regaining consciousness, Sara Williams was immediately gripped with a crippling sense of fear. The realisation that she had been taken was dawning on her and it made her blood run cold.

Her eyes were wide with fright, her heart palpitating so vigorously inside her chest that it felt as though it might burst through her chest. Her breathing was heavy and erratic, made even more punishing by the tape that was tightly sealed over her lips. The metallic taste of blood filled her mouth, her head was pounding from the numerous blows that rendered her unconscious and she could feel swelling on both sides.

The sheer terror that she was experiencing made her want to vomit and she felt the bile begin to rise from her empty stomach. She painfully swallowed it down, the motion uncomfortable against the dryness of her throat; she was *so* thirsty. Attempting to calm herself down but to no avail she succumbed to the anxiety. Her irregular breathing wouldn't subside, each sharp intake drawing in the scent of disinfectant that burned the inside of her nose. She was covered in a blanket of some sort which lay heavy on her body, stifling and claustrophobic. She wriggled around, trying to shrug it off which was made challenging by the fact that her wrists and ankles had been tied. She moved her head violently, wincing at the pain but managed to throw the blanket off, allowing herself to breathe a little easier.

Almost complete darkness greeted her, the only light was creeping around the edges of a rollout parcel shelf. She was in the back of a vehicle of sorts, she could feel it moving; each bump in the road making her head throb. She started to kick the interior of her place of confinement, hoping she would make enough noise that the driver would pull over. She struggled against her restraints, if he did pull over she wanted to be prepared. If she could just free her hands and feet, she could fight when the opportunity arose, the rope, however, just cut into her skin the more she pulled against it. Her attempts subsided quickly, her limbs starting to ache and she closed her eyes tightly.

She began to weep as she recalled the events that led to her current situation. She had been caught off guard, completely surprised by her captor. She could picture his face perfectly, as if he was still standing in front of her. He almost looked friendly but the feeling she got the moment she saw him was sinister. She remembered trying to run but he was fast, it had all happened so quickly, *too* quickly and now she had no idea where she was or where she was going.

Opening her eyes, her vision blurred from the tears, she tried to focus. Her eyesight had adjusted to the semi-darkness and, as her sobbing subsided, she tried to make out her cramped surroundings. She scanned the tiny space and, other than a small, dark holdall by her feet, it was bare. She shuffled her legs over and nudged the holdall onto its side; she could make out a couple of items, a roll of tape and what looked like a container of some variety. She allowed herself to relax a little, glad she hadn't discovered anything more threatening. Continuing to try and free herself from the rope, the soreness of the friction against her skin was becoming too much and she gave up, it was no use.

The vehicle slowed and made an abrupt, sharp turn and suddenly she was getting jerked around violently. She grimaced and yelped as her head bounced off the surface of the interior. Wherever they had turned wasn't a normal road, this felt like a far more rugged terrain. This part of the journey felt like an eternity due to the level of discomfort caused, she actually had no perceptible notion of time and had no idea how long she had been in the vehicle. They came to an unexpected and startling halt, the squeak of the brakes an unwelcome sound. Silence fell over the vehicle, as the ignition was turned off and she listened intently while the dread began to build once more. Listening carefully and purposefully, she heard the car door open and then slam shut, followed by gentle footsteps trudging along the side of the vehicle and stopping close to her prison. Silence once more. She stared closely at the door, her breathing increasing at such a rate that it made her throat hurt further. A few moments passed and then the door swung open, her eyes closed automatically at the shock of the sudden burst of natural light. She slowly opened her eyes and there he was, standing still, staring and smiling.

He leaned forward, 'Hello, Little Lamb.' He grinned again, grabbed her and roughly pulled her out of the vehicle and into his arms.

CHAPTER 7

Tapping the steering wheel along to the music on the radio, Michael couldn't stop smiling – it had all gone off without a hitch! His slender hand, slightly swollen from the beating he had administered, was beginning to throb painfully. The discomfort didn't bother him as much as the guilt of harming his 'Little Lamb' however. The memory of the incident wiped the smile from his face and he quickly pushed the thought from his mind. They were almost home and he was sure all would be well once they had the chance to talk.

The song on the radio ended and, in the short silence before the host started waffling, he could hear her struggling in the boot. *Thud, thud, thud...* He rolled his eyes, she was either going to hurt herself or damage his vehicle, he could do without either. Such a waste of energy too! Who would be able to hear her while they were driving along? Silly girl.

The journey was relaxing for him, after the exhilaration of this morning's events he needed this down time. It gave him the opportunity to collect his thoughts and devise a strategy of how to deal with her when they arrived at their destination. She was *not* going to be happy, he understood that but he had to be able to get her out and into the house without further harm. It was time to start repairing some of the damage he had done.

His mind wandered as he continued to drive down a remote country road and he almost missed his turn. Slamming on the brakes, he turned hard onto a dirt track that carved its way through a dense forest. He drove past a sign that said 'PRIVATE LAND', a deterrent he had placed there himself. The track was poorly looked after, bumpy and uneven, his 4x4 turbulently rocking from side to side as he proceeded along the route.

After a couple hundred yards, the rugged track ended and opened up into a more well maintained clearing. Within the clearing, a single building; an old farmhouse-style dwelling that had once belonged to his mother. Protected on all sides by towering Scots pine trees, the remote location was ideal.

He pulled up close to the house, applied the handbrake and switched off the engine. The silence that greeted him was gladly received and he used this moment of tranquillity to calm himself, the thudding in the back seemed to have subsided. He knew this next moment was possibly more important than the first time they met, just a short time earlier.

Taking a deep breath, he exited his 4x4 and closed the door behind him. He approached the rear of the vehicle cautiously and carefully, not wanting to startle her. He was nervous, her reaction wouldn't be a positive one, unsurprisingly. Wearing what was supposed to be a friendly grin, he opened the back door. Her eyes were closed initially but when she opened them, he could see the same terror as when they first met and it upset him. He tried taking the edge off by greeting her and smiling once more, before leaning in and pulling her into his arms.

Immediately, she began to struggle but he clamped her in a vice-like embrace, pressing his face against the top of her head and taking a deep breath of her scent. She continued to try and free herself from his grasp, her muffled screams growing increasingly panicked, but there was no way he was letting go of her now. Michael scooped her up so all of her weight was off the floor and began heading towards the house. This only served to increase her fighting, her legs flailing wildly, connecting with his shins and making him wince.

Nudging the front door open, daylight filled the dank, dusty hallway and he made for the stairs. Each step emitted a loud creak under their combined weight and his legs were beginning to tire, her unrelenting wriggling and duct tape stifled screams irritating him. He reached the top of the stairs, Sara still restrained in his arms, opened the first door to the left and threw her none-too-gently onto the old, dirty floorboards in the room.

'We will talk later, when you have calmed down!' he said, sternly.

Turning, he closed and locked the door, her anguished moans hurting him more than she could ever know. Skulking back down the staircase, his breathing heavy from the expenditure of energy to get her upstairs, he sighed. Her reaction was more than understandable, this wasn't exactly the traditional way to meet someone, but it didn't make it any less frustrating.

Reaching the bottom of the stairs, he walked out of the open front door and back to his vehicle which he ensured was shut and locked. Once he was certain, he headed back inside the house, ensuring the front door was also closed and locked behind him, before heading into the kitchen. Taking a seat at a small, beaten up dining table and rested his head in his hands. It had been a hectic morning and he was exhausted but at least he finally had her here. The next step was to try and explain to her why she was here and why he took her in the manner he did. Deciding he would allow her some time to cool off, he busied himself making her a snack to take up when the time was right. He just hoped that, when the moment came, he would be able to get her to see things from his point of view.

CHAPTER 8

Ambling across the street from where he had parked his car, a tired and dishevelled-looking Scott Harris approached the entrance to his favourite watering-hole. Reaching the door, he nudged it open and entered, the familiar scowl plastered across his handsome face.

Taking his place in his usual seat at the bar, he waited patiently for the barman to be finished with the customer he was serving before gesturing to get his attention.

'Double Glenlivet, please. Neat.' It was what he always ordered. Despite his Irish heritage, he *despised* their whisky, give him a good bottle of Scotch any day. While he waited for his drink to be poured and served to him, he took a moment to glance around at his surroundings. He liked it here, the atmosphere was friendly and if you wanted to socialise there were plenty of people who would oblige but if, like him, you just wanted to sit and drink alone, you wouldn't be pestered.

The barman placed his drink in front of him on top of a small napkin and walked away without taking payment – he knew it wouldn't be the only glass the detective would have. Scott frequented this place more often than he cared to admit, his dismal outlook on life causing him to habitually self-medicate. Picking up his drink, he sipped at it, savouring the fiery sensation as it burned his throat and warmed him from the inside.

'At least that's Monday done and dusted' he thought to himself, staring down into the amber liquid. He had successfully managed to finalise the two open cases he had left but he had found no joy in the accomplishment – the cases were dull, he needed some excitement, he needed a challenge. Scott hadn't always been this cynical, when he had been a young police officer walking the streets, he had savoured being involved in any case, no matter how small or uninteresting. These days, after working on many high profile investigations, the smaller cases lacked the ability to exhilarate him and fulfil his need for adrenaline. He swirled the whisky around in the glass before finishing it in one gulp and motioning for a refill.

Scott took a look around the bar once more, drinking it all in. The familiar din of indistinguishable chatter filled the room, smiling, happy faces and relaxed laughter giving the pub a warm, hospitable atmosphere. Just regular, happy-go-lucky individuals toasting the end of the most dreaded day of the week. The bar itself was nothing fancy, it was just your typical English pub; the clientele was an eclectic mix of people from all walks of life and professions and the ambiance was raucous and jovial. Scott couldn't have looked more out of place if he tried; his shoulders hunched and his brow furrowed, he looked exactly what he was: unapproachable.

Despite his external persona, he actually enjoyed the aura of the place but he really did savour the fact that he could enjoy it without anyone bothering him. No small talk, no pointless chit-chat, he could just sit and drink to the point of inebriation without being hounded and that was just how he liked it.

A sudden pang of self-pity washed over him, the alcohol starting to take effect and heightening his suppressed emotions. Was this what his life was now? Tedium, loneliness and a bottle of whisky? He gravely needed some stimulation, all aspects of his life, personal and professional, had become stale and he was becoming a miserable, old recluse. The biggest problem that he had was that he lacked the motivation and enthusiasm to make anything happen, he just wanted opportunities to fall into his lap. His second beverage arrived and he immediately took a large sip, desperately hoping that more alcohol would help to numb the bleak feelings he was experiencing.

As he stared down into the glass of whisky, watching the dim lights glinting off of the delicious liquid, he suddenly became aware of a presence next to him. Turning to his left, he looked into the big, hazel eyes of a very attractive woman; thick, dark hair tumbled effortlessly around her shoulders and her dark red lips were parted in a dazzling smile, showing straight, brilliant white teeth. Scott didn't return the smile, instead he looked a little perplexed.

'So, are you going to buy me a drink or what?' she said confidently, the large grin still etched across her striking face.

Scott pondered his response for a moment, trying to decide whether or not he could be bothered to put the effort in to have a meaningful interaction with this woman. Deciding against it, he dismissed her efforts. 'To be honest with you, love, you're wasting your time. I just want to be left alone.'

Undeterred and still smiling, she persisted, 'Oh come on, surely just one drink wouldn't hur-'

'What part of my previous sentence did you not *fucking* understand?' Scott interrupted, losing his patience and visibly annoyed by her insistence. 'Please, go *away.*'

Dejected and her large smile nowhere to be seen, the woman turned and walked away, leaving Scott alone once more with his drink and his thoughts.

The barman had been watching with interest and pretended to busy himself when Scott looked up at him. Taking another large glug of his whisky, Scott knew that his hostility towards the woman had been completely unwarranted. The problem he had these days was that he just lacked the energy and enthusiasm to socialise or entertain.

All the success over the years had led him to immerse himself more and more in his work and it had ended up taking the place of building any real relationships. Now, approaching forty, he was alone and it was beginning to dawn on him that it would probably remain that way. He sighed deeply, chugged the last of his drink and once again motioned for a refill. The realisation that he had wasted his life was becoming more obvious to him and the thought haunted him chronically.

CHAPTER 9

Groggily, she opened her eyes, rolled over and stared at the ceiling; the stains from old mould were obvious and they were smeared from a poor attempt at a clean up. Her eyes were sore from all the crying, the only time she could cease the tears flowing was when she slept. The new mattress she was laying on was actually quite comfortable, the fact that it was brand new alarmed her, he had clearly planned for this, he had been prepared. An uneaten sandwich was discarded on the grimy floor, an empty water bottle strewn alongside; the water had been gratefully received but her appetite was absent, how could she be expected to eat in this situation? Her stomach had been in a knot all day.

Standing up, she groaned out loud, her body sore from her ordeal. Slowly walking across the room, she reached the window and glanced outside. She realised she had slept for much longer than she anticipated; the sun had set, making way for the daunting darkness of the night. *He* had returned briefly, an hour or two after throwing her in this prison. When he opened the door and entered she had erupted, a wild frenzy of aggression but he had restrained her without difficulty – she was exhausted. She succumbed to him, too tired to continue fighting and in return he had removed the tape from her mouth. Her lips and the skin around her mouth were painfully sore from the adhesive and the relief was welcome. He had also removed the rope from her wrists and ankles, with the understanding that she remained calm. Involuntarily, she gently caressed the wounds created by her tethers. He had acted friendly, caring almost, and it had unnerved her. He had even tended to the injuries he had inflicted earlier that day; his hands being on her caused her to become hostile again and he upped and vacated without hesitation. It was almost like the confrontation was too much for him.

While alone, she had taken the opportunity to try and find a way out but it was to no avail. The door was locked, predictably, and the window was firmly sealed shut. Framed by old, dingy curtains, the window didn't allow for much of a view. She couldn't see all the way to the end of the track and the panorama was dominated by colossal trees acting like natural walls, confining her from the rest of the world. The room itself was barren, apart from the mattress she currently reclined on and a bucket in the corner for her... business. The walls were covered in old, drab wallpaper that was flaky and peeling and the wooden floorboards were coated in a generous layer of filth. Was this really going to be the last room she would see? Was she going to... *die* in here? The thought made her stomach churn.

Once again, she was swamped with a suffocating and debilitating sense of trepidation and she strolled back over to the mattress and laid down once more, pulling her knees up to her chest, assuming the foetal position. Holding herself tight, she began to shiver, the familiar sense of fear and helplessness rendering her incapacitated. Less than twenty-four hours ago, she was happy, she was content and she had been ripped away from her life. She began to cry, not for the first time that day and just prayed that she was being searched for already. Surely someone had realised she was missing? Her sobbing increased and the tears came thick and fast but there was no one to comfort her, she was alone, more alone than she had ever been and the feeling was terrifying.

CHAPTER 10

Picking up her phone, Janet Williams called her daughter a third time – voicemail, again. Since Sara had moved out, they had gotten into the routine of speaking on the phone at six o'clock each evening, without fail. It was now six minutes past the hour and each call attempt had gone straight to her voicemail – it didn't sit right.

She yelled to her husband, 'Peter! That's three times now, straight to voicemail!'

Peter emerged from the kitchen, a cup of tea in each hand and he passed one to his panic-stricken wife. 'She's probably had a busy day and forgotten to charge her phone, Janet. Please try to calm down.'

Janet smiled at her husband but it was a smile that didn't reach her eyes. She was worried, this wasn't like Sara at all. Peter watched as she raised the cup of tea to her lips and he could see she was shaking like a leaf. He reached over from his seat, removed the cup from her grasp and gently placed it on the coffee table.

'Please relax, love. She'll call.' His voice was calm and soothing but it did nothing to diminish her concern. She just nodded and tried to feign a calm demeanour but she knew something was wrong, a mother *always* knew. Janet had a unique relationship with her daughter, they were more like best friends and their relationship had always been comfortable and easy. She had always considered herself incredibly lucky when her friends complained to her about their unruly teenage daughters while she had a daughter who never caused her a days worry throughout her life. She grabbed her tea from the table, forcing herself to keep a steady hand and tentatively sipped at the hot liquid. She kept hold of the warm mug and cradled it in her lap before checking her phone once again – still nothing.

She knew that things were different now, Sara was a young woman with a career, her own friends and her own social life but that had never gotten in the way of their daily catch up before. Sara had always been responsible and aware of how certain actions would make her mother worry, so the fact that Janet hadn't heard from her at all, not even a message to let her know something had come up was incredibly out of character.

Janet just couldn't shake off the uneasy feeling, fighting a battle between her head and her heart; her head telling her that she was probably overreacting and her daughter was just out living her life, enjoying her independence, her heart was telling her that something had happened, that her daughter didn't ever go this long without some sort of communication. She could feel her husband still watching her and she tried to relax, tried to flush the worst-case scenario from her mind and be optimistic that Sara would be in touch soon, apologetic and promising to never make her worry again. She would give it a while longer but if she didn't hear anything soon, she was phoning the police.

CHAPTER 11

It was ten o'clock at night when DS Harris stumbled through his front door, a little wobbly from the copious amount of whisky he had consumed. He haphazardly kicked his shoes off and threw his jacket onto a hook before clumsily wandering into his kitchen. He filled a glass with water, his head spinning, and lapped it up eagerly, keen to lubricate his dry mouth. The cool water was refreshing and soothing and he immediately filled another glass before turning off the kitchen light and making his way along the hallway to the staircase.

As he lumbered, clumsily, up the stairs, his phone rang, the jingle startling him and causing him to spill water everywhere. Irritated, he fumbled around for his phone, pulled it out of his pocket and answered.

'DS Harris... Well how long has it been? No... Look, tell her to calm down and wait until morning. If she still hasn't heard from her, call back... Yes... Thank you. Goodnight.'

Annoyed, he finished his ascent of the stairs and headed for the bathroom to empty his bladder. An apparent missing girl, Sara Williams, probably out on the piss and making her parents worry – it happened all too often. What a fucking waste of time! He shook his head angrily, shocked that someone could think it was okay to call him with something so trivial.

He flushed the toilet and left without washing his hands, heading to his bedroom. He undressed as he walked across the room towards his bed, flinging clothes all over the place, further adding to the mess he lived in. He plugged his phone in to charge and the moment his head hit the pillow, he was out.

It was six a.m. when he woke up the next morning and his head was pounding – he really needed to lay off the whisky. He rolled over and picked up his phone, noticing five missed calls, all from his Superintendent. Scott groaned loudly, this many calls from his superior at this time of day did not bode well.

Calling back, the phone barely rang before Nick answered the phone.

'Where *THE FUCK* have you been?' Nick's voice shook with anger.

Scott muttered his apologies and listened intently as his boss explained the reason for his calls. Scott barely uttered a word other than the occasional murmur of agreement to show that he was listening. The girl hadn't been in touch with her parents overnight and they were beginning to think there was some substance to this. He was told Police Officers were meeting the parents at the girl's flat and he was to head there as well, post haste.

Before he even had the opportunity to vocalise his understanding to his superior, the phone line had already gone dead. Scott immediately felt guilty dismissing this last night but it was time to go and rectify that, hopefully there was a simple explanation. Hanging up, he hurriedly got dressed, grabbed what he needed and he was on his way.

CHAPTER 12

Arriving at the flat, there was already a lot of commotion. Scott parked his black BMW behind a patrol car and surveyed the scene; DC Lock's vehicle was parked in front of two patrol cars, a uniformed officer stood at the entrance to the flat and another was having a conversation with two people who, he could only assume, were the parents.

He got out of his car, taking the opportunity to smooth out his appearance using the reflection on the window and then walked toward the flat with intent. As he approached the open front door, he could feel the parents looking beyond the officer they were talking to and staring right at him, which made him feel a little uncomfortable. Had his cynicism the night before cost them precious time? He forced the thought from his mind, flashed his badge to the officer on the door and entered the flat.

DC Lock was already inside, deep in conversation with two more uniformed officers and Scott interrupted.

'What have we got so far?' he enquired. The two uniforms looked a little peeved by the sudden intrusion but took their leave and allowed their superiors some privacy.

'Not a lot so far, Sarge.' Lock responded. 'No signs of a struggle, no forced entry, no bags packed or items taken – nothing to tell us if she was either taken or left of her own accord.'

Scott nodded but didn't respond verbally and began his own search of the apartment. It was immaculately clean; the parquet flooring barely had a blemish, framed photos of family and friends hung proudly on the walls, giving the place a homely feel. In the kitchen there wasn't an item out of place, no unwashed dishes or old takeaway boxes like in his kitchen – she was definitely houseproud. He turned and exited the kitchen, wandering through to the living room. This room was also pristine, a large comfortable sofa adorned with cushions, carefully selected ornaments and trinkets gave the room some character and a large television mounted above a decorative mantel – nothing out of place again. As he made to leave the room, he noticed something that did seem a little odd: the curtains were pulled shut…

He mentally logged that observation and strolled through to the bedroom, still pondering the fact. As he walked in he noticed that it was the only room that actually showed any signs of life; an unmade bed and a creased t-shirt carelessly thrown on the floor. He was careful not to disturb anything but, again, mentally logged what he was seeing – anything and everything could be important in figuring out what had happened. Looking around the room, there wasn't much more to note but then his eyes were drawn to something on the back of the bedroom door. He pulled the door, almost shut, to take a look – hung on the back of the door was an outfit, a smart, stylish outfit, maybe laid out ready for work?

'Lock!' he yelled out into the hallway, the young man arriving in an instant.

'Sarge?'

'Get an officer to ask about her profession and see if she showed up to work yesterday.'

'No worries, Sarge.'

DC Lock hurried off while DS Harris stood waiting in the bedroom, this was important. This could help him start to establish a timeline. After several minutes, Lock returned.

'She never went to work, Sarge. Didn't call in sick or anything, just a no show!'

Scott walked past DC Lock and out into the hallway. 'Get forensics in here ASAP, see if there's anything in the bedroom; hair, fingerprints, anything!'

He continued towards the front door, planning on going to speak to some neighbours to ask if they had seen or heard anything. The parents stood, expectantly, at the front door and as he approached them noticed something else and stopped in his tracks. There were shoes lined up along the wall and there was, quite clearly, a pair missing – a set of muddy footprints confirming it. He knelt down for a closer look; trainers, he could tell from the tread. Looking up from his crouched position, he addressed the parents directly for the first time. Both looked worried but the Mother was ashen, a haunted look in her tired eyes.

'Does your daughter run in the mornings?' he queried.

Both parents nodded, nervously.

'Does she run nearby?'

They both nodded again, not uttering a word.

'Take me there, *now*.'

CHAPTER 13

At the park, Scott stood alone absorbing his surroundings. Large trees guarded all sides of the park, except for the entrance, restricting vantage points from any of the residential buildings. The entrance side was more open, too open and wouldn't allow for any surprises. He couldn't figure out a way she could disappear from here.

More uniforms had arrived and helpful neighbours and residents had joined to help scour the park, with strict instructions not to touch anything they might find. None of these neighbours had seen her come or go the previous morning and she hadn't arrived at work. There were no signs at all, it was like she had just *vanished*.

In typically British fashion, the weather had taken a turn for the worse in the time they had been at the park, it was cold and a freezing wind swirled around them, the trees swaying with the strength of the gusts. The rain that had accompanied the wind, although light, was strengthened by the gale and it harshly whipped against the side of his face.

He watched as officers and members of the public worked harmoniously, searching for clues. Sara's parents were huddled close together, a few metres from where he stood. He had advised against them helping with the search, telling them that their emotional state could affect their concentration, a view they had accepted. The truth was, if they stumbled across something sinister, the damage it would do could be irreversible.

While the group of officers and members of the public continued the search, he took the opportunity to walk the route she may have run. His footsteps made a gentle splash in the water that was beginning to pool on the surface of the path, his eyes constantly sweeping the floor, searching for any sign that she had made it here. He walked slowly, focussed and determined. Rounding the final corner, where the path ran parallel to the small woodland, he began inspecting the undergrowth. Suddenly, his concentration was disturbed.

'WE HAVE SOMETHING!' one of the uniformed officers yelled at the top of his voice, from the area Scott was heading towards. He broke into a sprint along the path, unaware that he was mirroring exactly what Sara had done the previous morning.

He reached the officer, who was holding up a solitary earring in a gloved hand. Scott called The Williams over, needing to see if they recognised the item. They answered his call and trudged toward him, cutting across the damp grass rather than using the path. Their walk was cautious and laboured and it felt like an eternity until they were in front of him. Scott took the earring in his own gloved hand and presented it to Sara's parents; Janet's eyes widened and she burst into tears, her uncontrollable, hysterical cries answered the question he hadn't even had the chance to ask. Her knees buckled and her husband caught her, pulling her close, muffling her distressed sobs.

Scott motioned to an officer to take them away and as he did so, he noticed an area of trodden down foliage just inside the perimeter of the small woods. Venturing into it, he could see it was freshly squashed. Pushing a little further in, he could make out a discernible path, which he followed. He carefully examined the route as he traipsed along it, there were obvious areas of stomped earth and shrubbery but no clear footprints. The path ended at an opening; a quiet, public area, perfect for a concealed getaway. His heart was pounding – had he found where she was taken?

Turning back, he phoned DC Lock to request forensics to be sent over to take photos and inspect the area more thoroughly. As he emerged back into the park, he was greeted by a friendly looking, almost awkward gentleman. The stranger's face lit up at the sight of DS Harris.

'I heard about the missing girl, is there anything I can do to help? He smiled as he asked the question.

Scott was a little caught off guard by the sudden appearance of this man but replied politely; 'We're all set thank you and I'll have to ask you to vacate the area, it has just become a crime scene.'

The man looked a little dejected and shifted uncomfortably before smiling and accepting the response. 'OK, no worries Officer.'

Scott smiled curtly and escorted the man to the exit of the park, eager to build on what he had found. The man gave a small, polite wave and Scott watched him walk away before looking back into the park, unknowingly turning his back on the man who had caused it all.

CHAPTER 14

Entering his flat, Michael took off his coat and carefully hung it up. With shaking hands, he clumsily unbuttoned the shirt he was wearing and allowed his sweaty body to breathe. He was exhilarated, what on earth had possessed him to do that? His heart was beating a mile a minute, the excitement giving him butterflies; he had never felt so powerful, so in control and the feeling was as satisfying as it was bewildering.

Slipping off his shoes and placing them neatly in the hallway, he glided into the kitchen to make himself some tea. He filled the kettle with precisely enough water to make one cup and flicked the switch to start the boiling process. Grabbing a cup from the cupboard, he placed it gently on the work surface and threw in a tea bag. While he waited for the kettle to boil, he allowed himself a moment to relax and catch his breath. He had been impulsive this morning and he had to try and control those sudden urges, mistakes would be costly in this situation.

Seeing the commotion at Sara's flat as he drove past had been too alluring, however, and he had decided to act the part of concerned, helpful resident. Unfortunately, he had been too late to join the actual search, which seemed to be wrapping up when he arrived but he had spoken to a detective! A man who would, no doubt, be searching for him and he had spoken to him! He had stood right in front of him and the detective was none the wiser. Laughing out loud, Michael relished the hilariousness of the irony. The man they would all be looking for had stood eye to eye with a detective and nobody had a clue! Oh, he felt so alive!

The kettle boiled and he gently saturated the tea bag and left it to soak for a moment. For once, not being noticed hadn't left a bitter taste in his mouth – it had finally worked in his favour! His whole childhood was tainted by foster families who had only acknowledged his existence when they abused him. Because of this, blending in had become his forte. He lied to himself, believing it was a choice but his silent, eccentric personality tended to repel people; deep down all he wanted was to be noticed, recognised as a human being. The only person who had ever cared about him had taken her own life and left him on his own. A selfish act by his mother which had left him to fend for himself among people who saw him as nothing less than a smear on their lives. He shook these sad thoughts from his mind, he had Sara now and she would learn to love him, eventually she would see what a great person he was.

He removed the tea bag from the cup, placed it in the bin and added a generous amount of milk to the vessel before eagerly sipping at the concoction. After yesterday's events, today would pale in comparison as he had to return to his normal life. Michael worked, part-time, at a convenience store; it paid just enough for him to live and would also allow him to continue his 'extra-curricular' activities – how convenient! He wanted nothing more than to just return to his 'Little Lamb' but this facade needed to be maintained in order to protect himself and his love.

This whole plan had been meticulous; he had watched Sara for months, studied her, learned her life. He knew where she lived, where she worked, where she exercised, he had even watched her socialise with friends and family. He had to ensure he knew her habits and the way she lived before he took her. It was extremely important that he had put the man hours in to organise everything effectively; the less evidence, the higher chance he would get away with it – which, in turn, would give him the time he needed to show Sara how much he cared about her. 'The two most powerful warriors are patience and time' he thought to himself, quoting *War and Peace*.

Finishing his tea, he washed the cup and put it back in the cupboard, leaving the kitchen spotless as always. He wandered through to his bedroom for a change of clothes, his perspiration had soiled these ones. Removing his shirt and trousers he opened his wardrobe to select a new outfit, almost identical to the one he had just removed. Once clothed, he headed back out into the hallway, put on his shoes and a fresh jacket and left for work.

As he strolled in the fresh, autumn air, he felt content. For the first time in a long time he felt as though things were going his way. Although yesterday had been difficult, he knew it was the only way to do it – a girl like her wouldn't be interested in him in a million years! But now, he had the time and the opportunity to show her how well he could treat her.

His walk to work was brief but enjoyable, the gentle breeze refreshing and invigorating. Completely lost in his own thoughts, the world around him was a blur, he felt at ease – a few hours of work, of normality and he could get back to what really mattered.

As he entered the store, the owner, an elderly gentleman called Jim Hartfield greeted him with a familiar look of disdain which went straight over his head. Jim was a grumpy old sod, short and balding, the few hairs that were scattered on his head a bright silver. Jim didn't like being around this weirdo but he was so bloody organised! The store ran like clockwork with him here so he tolerated his presence. Michael gave Jim an amiable grin and wandered through to the back of the store. He placed a navy waistcoat, which bore the store name, over his shirt, fastened his nametag on the breast and walked back out into the store.

Jim was restocking shelves and Michael took his place behind the counter, ready to greet any customers.

'You hear about that missing girl?' Jim asked suddenly, clearly just making small talk but the unexpected question startled Michael.

He hid his discomfort well and replied. 'Yes, very sad. Very sad indeed.'

'Apparently the police are holding a press conference later, on national TV. Hopefully good news!'

Panic coursed through Michael's body, a *national* press conference? This was too soon, he hadn't expected this level of attention so quickly. Had they found something? Was this going to be over before it had even begun? He didn't bother responding to Jim, his mind was racing. He tried to clear his head and force himself to calm down, there was absolutely no point in worrying yet. He would just have to wait and see what the point of this was. Just a few hours to get through and he could return to his 'Little Lamb.' He would worry about the press conference when the time came.

CHAPTER 15

Standing alone in the police station's smoking area, Scott finished a cigarette, stubbed it out, discarded the butt and immediately lit another. He was trying to placate the feeling of stress he was confronted with, today had been overwhelming. After the events of the morning, the realisation that he had been wrong and the young woman had been abducted, he now had to conduct a press conference, a press conference that was going to be broadcast on bloody national television! It had been several years since he had worked on a case of national interest, the high profile nature was only going to increase the pressure he was under – he was nervous. The irony that he had been hoping for a more exciting case and then this had happened, was not lost on him either. He put his second cigarette to his lips and inhaled deeply, the tip glowing bright orange as he did so. Holding the smoke in his lungs for a moment, he allowed the nicotine to take effect before exhaling through his nose and mouth, ejecting the smoke into the evening air.

He hadn't felt this tense in a long time, he was concerned that he may have allowed his cynical nature to have an effect on the case. More importantly, it may have an effect on the young woman's life. He shouldn't have been so dismissive when he got the phone call and he regretted his actions immensely, he just hoped he would get the opportunity to rectify his mistake.

It had been close to thirty-six hours since Sara had gone missing, the first seventy-two hours usually being pivotal in cases like this, and they had nothing substantial to go on. They had one of her earrings, which at least told them she had been at the park and they had the woodland which showed all the signs of her being taken through there. Unfortunately, that was it, they had nothing that could give them an idea of where she had been taken or by whom.

Forensics had taken all afternoon to search the park and the woodland, leaving no stone unturned. On the plus side, they had found nothing sinister; no blood, no signs of any injury or worse, *death*. On the down side, finding nothing meant they didn't have a single thing that would help the case, it was going to take some good, old fashioned detective work to solve this one. The thought made him chuckle but it wasn't a happy laugh, he knew what he was really going to need was a big, fat stroke of luck. They had questioned neighbours, residents, anyone who even walked through the area and no one had seen or heard a thing. With forensics coming up empty as well, they had to go national, make the case big news and see if it gave them something, *anything*.

Stubbing out his second cigarette and aggressively throwing it on the floor, he crouched down and buried his head in his large hands. He had roughly half an hour before the press conference, before he had to ask the public to help him do his job. He was still hunched down when he felt a hand on his shoulder, which gave him a jolt. Looking up from his squat, he saw that the hand belonged to DC Lock. Scott stood up and addressed his colleague, 'Lock.'

'Sarge' he paused. 'You all good?'

'Do I fucking look all good?' Scott snapped impatiently.

Lock stepped back, his concerned expression changing to one of indignation. He turned to walk away but Scott grabbed his shoulder and apologised.

'I'm sorry, mate, that was uncalled for. It's been a long fucking day, you know?' His voice was a mixture of exasperation and entreatment.

Lock smiled understandably, 'No harm, Sarge. They're almost ready inside.'

Scott nodded his thanks and DC Lock went back inside with Scott following soon after.

Once inside, Scott made a detour to the bathroom where he promptly vomited in the sink, unable to make it to the toilet. Today had really taken its toll on him but he had to get a hold of himself, be confident and in control. He didn't want The Williams to see him to see him in this state, they had to believe he could solve this. *He* had to believe he could solve this, he had never doubted his ability to solve a case before but the fact that he was blaming himself for this was having a negative effect on his usual self-belief. Turning on both taps, he rinsed his puke away, then swirled some water in his mouth before spitting it out, he then washed his hands and splashed some cold water on his face. Drying himself off, he stared at his reflection in the mirror – he looked rough. Fortunately for him, he had managed to find the time to pop home and change into a good suit before the press conference – he hoped his attire might help draw some of the attention away from his face. Reaching into his jacket pocket, he pulled out a pack of chewing gum and chucked a couple of pieces into his mouth, needing the mintiness to eliminate the mixed scent of smoke and sick. Chewing frantically, he left the bathroom and marched down the corridor, he could hear the gentle hubbub caused by the media assembling in the conference room and tried to ignore it.

As he reached the end of the corridor, he turned right and entered a room that was attached to the conference room. Walking in, he looked around; DC Lock was already there and he nodded in his direction. His Superintendent, Nick Wilson, was there as well quietly talking to The Williams, outlining how the press conference was going to go. Scott knew all too well how this went; Nick would say a few words and introduce him, Scott would then have to outline his thoughts and the intent of the investigation. The Parents would then get an opportunity to say something. That was always the hardest part for Scott, seeing innocent people thrust into the media spotlight to plead for the safe return of their loved one. Finally, the media would get the opportunity to ask questions – he absolutely despised that part, journalists were abhorrent, insensitive vultures whom he had very little time for.

Taking a seat in the corner of the room, he closed his eyes and took a long, deep breath, trying to calm his nerves. He just had to get this out of the way and he could get back to his investigation – he had *a lot* to do. He would immerse himself in this case, as he had always done, it would become the most important thing in his life. This case, in particular, he had to give everything he had – the guilt he was experiencing was consuming him. Back in the day he would never have acted that way but he had allowed his own personal issues to dictate his response to a case and if the worst happened, he would never forgive himself.

His thoughts were suddenly interrupted by Nick's voice. 'We're on, Scott. Let's go.' He didn't wait for Scott's response, he just walked through to the conference room, followed closely by The Williams. Scott stared at them as they walked past, they both looked drawn and exhausted, this day had probably been the worst of their lives. Scott got up from his seat and went through, Nick was showing The Williams to their seats at the table in front of the media. Scott took his seat next to them, so they were to his left and Nick took the final empty seat to Scott's right.

The din created by the chatter of the various members of the media died down and silence fell over the room, the only sound was the multiple camera shutters from photographers. Several video cameras were positioned front and centre, ready to broadcast live to multiple news channels around the country. Nick had already started saying his part but Scott wasn't paying attention, he was going over what he was going to say in his head – it was time to step up. Once again, his thoughts were punctuated by his superior's voice.

'... Our lead investigator, Detective Sergeant Scott Harris.'

Scott could feel all eyes turn to him as he leaned towards his microphone, camera shutters continuing to go off at an increasing rate.

'Thank you, Superintendent Wilson' he started and nervously cleared his throat. 'After the initial stages of our investigation, we have strong reason to believe that Miss Williams was abducted yesterday morning, whilst on a run, somewhere between six and six-thirty a.m.' He paused and took a large gulp of water from the glass that was in front of him. 'We know she left for a run, as was her routine on week-days but we have also been able to ascertain that she did not return from that run. She didn't show up for work, she didn't have her daily phone call with her Mother-' a sudden whimper from Janet Willaims interrupted him but he continued. 'We ask you, the public, especially those of you from the local area, to come forward if you think you know something or saw something… no matter how trivial it may seem.' He stopped again and, gesturing toward the photo of Sara that was pinned on the board behind him, con-cluded his address. 'Sara is described as five foot six, athletic build and she would've been wearing active-wear or running clothes of some variety. As you can see from her photo, she has blonde hair and green eyes. Please, take a long look at this picture and if you think you may have information which could help us, don't hesitate to call – time is of the essence.'

Sinking back into his seat, he gulped thirstily at his remaining water – his throat was as dry as a bone. Glad his part was over, he allowed himself to relax a little. He half-listened as Nick introduced The Williams so they could plead for the safe return of their daughter. Scott tried to shut out the anguished tones of the Father's voice while he spoke, Janet's hysterical sobs increasing throughout. It made Scott sick to the stomach, these poor people on live television, begging a stranger to let their daughter come back to them. He was determined to find her *alive* – the alternative wasn't an option for him.

He grew distressed, the emotion of the situation getting to him and when he heard Nick open the floor to questions, he stood up and left. He placed an affectionate hand on Janet's shoulder and then Peter's, before marching from the conference room. He would get it in the neck from Nick later but he didn't care, he had an investigation to run and a young woman to find.

CHAPTER 16

Sara stood at the window of her prison and stared out into the darkness. The weather had calmed and the large Scots Pine trees that surrounded her stood tall and motionless, like the Queen's Guard outside Buckingham Palace. She had never felt so alone, so hopeless – the solitude was gruelling. *He* had left her the night before, after her outburst and he hadn't returned. It was almost worse than when he was actually there, the confinement played with her imagination and increased her fear. The duration of his absence raised so many questions in her mind. Where had he gone? What was he doing? Why had he taken her and then just left her here on her own? What would he do when he came back? She wasn't even sure she actually wanted the answers to these questions, it could be something far more sinister than her mind could possibly fabricate.

Sara was exhausted, the constant, acute sense of peril was draining her energy and she had no distractions, nothing to stop her mind wandering into the worst case scenario. Her stomach rumbled, she had barely eaten – only consuming the sandwich he left once she finally succumbed to the hunger pains in her stomach. By the time she had gotten around to eating it, it was stale and it hurt her jaw to chew. She raised a hand to her face and tentatively caressed the swelling on her cheek from one of the punches, her head still pounding from the battering she had taken.

Being alone all day had given her the opportunity to ponder over the circumstances surrounding her current situation and it had only led to more confusion. The level of aggression he had shown when he took her was terrifying, violence seemed to come to him easily and with little hesitation. However, once here, he seemed passive, almost timid and when she had tried confronting him he had taken the opportunity to leave without causing her further harm. It was almost as if he was two different people.

She also had no idea why she was here, why she had been taken or who he was. She knew that in most abductions the perpetrator was known to the victim but after a full day of racking her brain, digging deep into her memory, she had come up with nothing – she had definitely never seen him before! Was she just a victim of opportunity? No. He had been too prepared, too relaxed throughout – he had this planned. There were too many questions and the fact that she couldn't answer any of them frustrated her.

Her brainstorm was interrupted by the sudden appearance of headlights coming down the dirt track. She pressed herself close to the window, her palms flat against the cold glass – had someone found her? Had someone come for her? Was this nightmare going to be over? Her pulse quickened as she watched the approaching vehicle, the headlights making her squint as it got closer.

The vehicle pulled into the clearing in front of the house and her heart plummeted – it was *him*. Now it was closer, she could just about make out the shape of the car through the shadows, as it slowly trundled towards the house. Again, she was filled with terror, wondering if this was it, if her death was imminent. She knew how it worked, she had seen these situations unfold on the news and there was never a happy ending.

She watched with apprehension as the 4x4 pulled up and saw him get out of the vehicle. He looked straight up at her and smiled, sending a chill down her spine. She retreated to her mattress and cowered in the corner, her body trembling with trepidation and her stomach twisted in a knot. Listening intently, she heard the front door groan open and bang shut, the sound of a set of keys jostling echoed up the stairs. Footsteps followed, slow and heavy, each loud scuff on every step striking terror into her soul, the volume increasing as he got closer. The footsteps stopped and she stared at the door, she listened as the keys rattled again and then the door swung open. He stood in the doorway staring straight at her, a 'bag for life' in each hand. Sara closed her eyes tight, she didn't want to know what those bags contained. She listened as he closed the door and locked it, then footsteps and the rustling of bags as he approached her. Her breathing was panicked and erratic and as she inhaled she caught a scent... a pleasant scent. Opening her eyes cautiously, he stood at the end of her mattress, holding out a crammed carrier bag that he held outstretched in her direction.

'Chinese?' he smiled.

Adjusting her position, she sat up a little and looked at him warily.

'I wasn't sure what you liked so I just bought a selection' he said cheerfully, unbagging the food. 'I thought we could eat and maybe watch a little something?'

Sara didn't respond, her eyes moving back and forth from the food to his face. Why was he being so friendly? It creeped her out... but... she was *so* hungry! He sauntered back across the room to the other bag, reached in and produced an iPad. Turning back and heading towards her, he sat on the far end of the mattress and then gestured towards the food he had laid out; 'Eat, please.'

Shuffling forward a touch, not taking her eyes from him, she reached out and picked up one of the food containers. Ripping the lid off, the glorious sight of spring rolls greeted her and she grabbed one and bit into it eagerly. She could feel his eyes on her the entire time and noticed him visibly relax when she began to eat – he started to tuck in, himself. Sara was ravenous and she shoved a second spring roll in her mouth and lunged forward for the chow mein, shovelling in mouthfuls with a plastic fork. While she stuffed her face, still vigilantly watching him, he set up the iPad and turned it on to a news stream. It took a few moments to load but when it did, she dropped the food all over the floor. As she stared at the screen, her own face looked back at her – she was on the news! The news anchor was talking about how she had gone missing, presumably abducted and a press conference was due to commence shortly. Sitting forward, she was transfixed and she watched intently as it cut to live pictures of an empty table with four microphones placed on it. A man walked into the shot, identified as Police Superintendent Nick Wilson, followed by… her parents! They looked awful! Her mum looked like she had aged ten years and her dad looked gaunt and dishevelled; her eyes filled with tears as she watched them hold each other, Sara looked across at the man who had caused all this pain and could see he was watching as intently as her, was he... *worried?* Turning back to the news, the superintendent had just introduced the lead investigator, Detective Sergeant Scott Harris. A fleeting sense of optimism flowed through her body, they were taking her disappearance very seriously! With this many people looking for her, surely it was only a matter of time before she was found? She just hoped he kept her alive long enough...

As the sergeant spoke, however, it became more apparent that they had very little to go on. They were certain she had been taken but they had no suspects and they were asking the public to help, *please* let there be someone who saw something. This news was clearly music to her captors ears as he was grinning like a Cheshire cat, her optimism disappeared as quickly as it had arrived. She slumped back against the wall, defeated – they had *nothing*. No one knew where she was, no one knew who had taken her and she was stuck here with a creep who would probably end her life and bury her in the forest outside. The thought made her feel sick to her stomach.

She sat and watched as the Detective finished his part and the camera focussed on her parents. Her mother, inconsolable, said nothing but her dad spoke to the camera, his voice breaking.

'Please, please, if you have Sara, please don't hurt her. She's our little girl, our only child.' Her dad paused, taking a moment to gather himself. 'Please, just let her go, let her come home. We don't even need to press charges, we don't even have to know who you are, we just want our daughter ba-' his voice cracked and he burst into tears, Sara cried with him, her body shaking violently as she struggled to catch her breath between sobs.

Her captor turned off the ipad and spun round to face her, his face full of glee.

'Do you see that?' he asked rhetorically. 'We're famous, Little Lamb.'

CHAPTER 17

November 2016

Parking his BMW in his usual spot outside the station, a tired and scruffy looking Scott Harris stepped out of his vehicle into the brisk November air and lit a cigarette. He had time for a brief moment of respite before another exasperating day. Avidly sucking at his cigarette, he enjoyed the calm before the inevitable chaos. This case was sucking the life out of him but he had no choice but to persevere, his tenacity was what had made him so successful in the past. Having one final drag on his cigarette, he threw it to the ground half finished, the embers still burning away on the floor. Reaching back inside his car, he gathered up a stack of files that had been strewn on the passenger seat, and made his way to the station entrance.

Storming through the front doors, he bumped into someone without acknowledging their presence and unapologetically continued his march towards his place of work. He reached the security doors and awkwardly juggled the stack of files whilst struggling to enter the code in the keypad, cursing as he input the code incorrectly with his first try. Finally getting through the doors, he adjusted the files before they spilled from his arms and walked towards his destination with intent.

A room had been specifically set up for the abduction case and, ignoring the existence of any of his colleagues, he entered the room, slamming the files down on a vacant table. DC Lock was already there, feverishly looking through witness statements and he looked up, startled by the sudden commotion. Looking at Scott, he could see the effect the case was having on him; his persistent scowl was now accompanied by dark rings around his eyes, his facial hair had grown long and scraggly and his suit was creased. Looking closer, Lock could tell that it was the same suit as the day before.

A month had passed since Sara Williams went missing and they weren't any closer to a lead than they were four weeks prior. They had worked tirelessly, almost every day since but Scott had taken it to another level; he hadn't had a single day off, despite warnings from both his colleagues and his superiors. Getting burnt out wasn't going to help anyone but it seemed he had taken this case personally, he was obsessed; taking work home and never giving himself time to relax.

Scott caught Lock staring at him. 'Don't look at me like that, mate. I know I look like shit, I don't need to be told that I look like shit.' He removed his jacket, placed it on the back of a chair and slumped down into it, behind the table where he had thrown his files.

'Did you... sleep in your suit, Sarge?' Lock enquired, cautiously.

Scott fired him a look that was enough of a response to the question and Lock silently returned to his work.

Scott, satisfied that Lock would leave him alone for a while, pulled a file from the top of the large pile, opened it and started to read. He had been back out to Sara's neighbourhood and re-interviewed residents, hoping a second round of questioning might jog a memory. He hadn't had much luck but he had decided to go through all the written statements again, hoping something would suddenly jump out at him. They were clutching at straws, he knew that, but they had to remain optimistic and trust the process. The problem was, it seemed like whoever had taken Sara was a fucking ghost! They had nothing even close to a suspect, not a single person of interest whatsoever and without a lead, Scott knew they would be on borrowed time – the chances of them finding the missing girl alive decreased with every day that passed.

They had already come under heavy scrutiny in the national press – one of the downsides to a case of this nature. The public wanted answers and the press fed that hunger, which wasn't particularly helpful. When the Chief of Police had gotten wind of the negative press he had come down hard on the department, in particular his Superintendent Nick Wilson. A meltdown from Nick had followed which had only increased the pressure they were feeling and, in turn, increased the level of stress.

Scott still blamed himself, constantly wondering whether they would be at a more positive stage in this case if he had taken it seriously a little sooner. He closed the file he had finished reading – nothing of note in that one. This would probably be a pattern as he continued rooting through these statements but he would persevere and he grabbed a second file, praying he got a break. Never, throughout his whole career, had he had a case like this; one with zero helpful evidence or a witness.

They had been able to establish a sequence of events from the kidnapping and knew that it had been planned and planned well, crimes of opportunity tended to leave *something* behind. The abductor, however, had clearly known where she lived, where she ran, where he could watch her and take her without being noticed. It had been executed perfectly, something Scott hated to admit but they had been left with absolutely nothing to go on. He slammed the second file shut, shoved it to the side and sat back in his seat already getting irritated.

They knew Sara had left her flat for a run, they had evidence that confirmed her arrival at the park and signs of where the kidnapper had waited and where he had gotten away. The question they still couldn't answer was what happened next? It was almost like they had vanished into thin air.

Casting his eye around the room, ignoring Lock who had glanced up at him, he realised how pathetic it really looked. Anyone looking from the outside in must think they're a joke! They had set up three mobile whiteboards to document the case as it progressed and they hadn't even filled the first one, the emptiness of the other two stood out horribly. The few pieces of the puzzle they had found looked lonely on the first whiteboard and he averted his eyes.

The fear Scott had now, a thought he was keeping to himself, was that Sara was already dead. It kept him up at night, the thought that this case would eventually just lead to a body, discarded like old rubbish in a shallow grave, like so often was the case in disappearances. The difference this time was that he felt partly responsible, he had dismissed the initial call and potentially cost them precious time. But, even though he blamed himself, he blamed the unknown perpetrator more. How anyone could do that to another human was beyond him, how someone could destroy so many lives and tear families apart. Battling the morbid thoughts, he continued to tell himself she *was* still alive and he was going to find her – he just had to keep digging and hope for a stroke of luck. He had to be confident in his own ability to solve this case, after all, his track record spoke for itself. He knew he was once a good detective, he just had to *believe* he could find that old spark once more.

For so long he had complained his job had become dull, that he wanted a proper case to work on and here it was, he had an opportunity to prove he still had it in him. He rubbed roughly at his tired eyes, sat forward and grabbed another statement. This girl's life was hanging in the balance and he wasn't going to let her down.

CHAPTER 18

Slumping down into the sofa, Peter Williams removed his shoes and sighed loudly. He had just returned from another walk around the park and woodland where his daughter had gone missing, something he had done every day since her abduction. He knew it was optimistic and, more accurately, a little delusional but he thought if he continued to explore the area, he might come across something that would help bring his daughter home. It was unlikely the police had missed anything, he knew that, but being somewhat proactive made him feel better. The feeling was temporary, however, as soon as he was alone with his thoughts the optimism would disappear.

Sitting forward, Peter rested his head in his hands and closed his eyes. The stress was unbearable and the feeling of utter uselessness was eating him alive, knowing that his walks were merely a way of making himself feel as though he was making a difference. As a father, he felt responsible for his daughter's safety and he hadn't been able to look after her.

It had been a month since their daughter had been ripped from their lives and Janet had fallen apart in that period. Each day she would get steadily worse; disconsolate and despairing, she had eventually stopped leaving their home and spent most of the day bed-ridden and unapproachable. It didn't stop Peter trying though and he would go up and talk to her each day. She had barely spoken since Sara's disappearance and getting her to eat and drink had become troublesome. Perseverance and a gentle, caring approach were key and Peter managed to get her to eat a little something most days. He tried remaining strong and hopeful for both of their sakes but the emotional responsibility laid heavily on his shoulders and was beginning to wear him down. His wife had become a shadow of her former self, almost unrecognisable to the woman he had married forty years ago. It was painful for him to see the woman he loved deteriorate this way and, although he understood her decline, he found his duties as a supportive husband becoming increasingly onerous. It almost felt as though they were going through this ordeal completely individually and it bothered him.

Janet's mental collapse shouldn't have really come as a surprise to him, the relationship she had with her daughter was truly unique. They were more like best friends than mother and daughter, a connection which had left him feeling pushed aside at times. He hadn't ever let it bother him, however, it had actually warmed his heart to see how happy and content they were in each other's presence. In his eyes, he had a perfect little family and he was the luckiest man on earth.

This feeling hadn't come about without their fair share of hard times and this wasn't the first time Peter and Janet had been through a tragedy together. They had been expecting before they had Sara, several years before. They had been ecstatic when they found out, they were wildly in love and eager to start a family but five months into the pregnancy, Janet had suffered a miscarriage and their whole world had come crashing down around them. Not only did they lose their baby, a little boy, but due to complications from the miscarriage, they were told their chances of conceiving in the future were almost zero. The news was a sucker punch and their elation had turned to misery. Janet fell into a deep depression and Peter spent every waking moment trying to find a way to 'fix' them. It had been a long road to recovery, for the both of them, but eventually they had managed to come to terms with the hand they had been dealt. Gradually they got back on track, slowly their wounds healed and they had built a wonderful, fulfilling marriage. Years later, a surprise, completely out of the blue – Janet had fallen pregnant. Against all odds, she was with child again but they were cautious, rather than exuberant and they approached the gestation period with open minds. Nine nerve-wracking months passed in the blink of an eye and they were rewarded with a child; a beautiful, miraculous, little baby girl. Their world was complete.

A stray tear rolled down Peter's cheek and he quickly wiped it away, stifling the sudden rush of sadness and nostalgia. A little over a month ago, he was a content husband and father, his daughter was flourishing and his wife couldn't have been happier. Fast forward to the present day and his perfect world had been torn apart and he didn't know how to repair it this time. If they didn't find Sara, he didn't know how they would recover.

In typical fashion, he suppressed these thoughts and feelings, stood up and walked from the living room to the kitchen. Flicking the switch on the kettle, he grabbed two mugs and placed a teabag in each. He stood and watched the kettle as the liquid began to effervesce and steam gently creep out of the spout. Once the water had boiled, he distributed it equally into each mug and allowed it to brew for a moment before adding a splash of milk to both and Janet's usual three sugars to hers. Once completed, he began his ascent upstairs and headed for the bedroom.

Janet was awake but lay under the duvet staring at the wall, unblinking. Peter stood in the doorway for a moment, almost hesitant to continue his approach and looked at his wife. Janet looked awful, he hated thinking it but it was the truth. Her eyes were gaunt and dark, the product of very little quality sleep over the span of a month. Her hair was untamed and unwashed, her facial expression was haunted and vacant. Peter's heart broke seeing his beautiful soulmate looking this way, knowing there was only one way to solve it but also knowing it was out of his hands. The police were working hard and he had to put his trust in them.

Clutching both mugs of tea, he delicately approached his wife, placed her tea on the bedside table and then perched on the edge of the bed.

'I made you a cup of tea, love' he said caringly.

Silence.

'Love? I made you a cup of tea, three sugars – just the way you like it' he tried again.

Janet didn't move, didn't acknowledge him at all, it was as if she was completely unaware of his presence. He quietly sipped his tea, he could feel the frustration building inside him and tried to ignore it – he would just give her a minute. Her gaze hadn't deviated from the empty space that she was staring into, the only movement coming from the gentle motion of her body as she breathed. A few minutes passed and getting impatient, Peter gave her a gentle nudge – still no response and he snapped.

'For Christ's sake, Janet, will you talk to me? You're not the only one going through this!'

That did it, Janet slowly rotated onto her back and pulled herself upright so she sat looking at him. Her eyes, full of disdain, were burning into his.

'I don't feel like pandering to your needs right now, Peter. Why don't you go on another one of your aimless walks?' She said it calmly but the tone was unnerving. 'My daughter-' she started.

'*Our* daughter' he corrected.

Janet continued, unflinching '-is missing, Peter, I don't feel like talking or getting up or DRINKING THIS FUCKING TEA!' She bellowed and picking up the full mug of tea from the bedside table, threw it against the wall, the porcelain shattering and the brown liquid splashing everywhere.

Peter stood up, shocked at the sudden outburst, the surprise evident on his face. He could see the anger in his wife's face and her hands shaking, he stood silently while she continued.

'I have carried two babies in my life Peter, *two!* And as of this moment, I have neither of them. I grew them inside myself, in *my* body and I have been unable to successfully look after either!' She was bawling, tears gushing down her face like tiny waterfalls. 'My body created them and now I have nothing to show for it, so *please* don't pretend that we're going through the same thing. You have no idea how I feel, you'll never know!' She stopped, still weeping, her breathing erratic and the words hung heavy in the air between them. They stared at each other for a few moments before Peter turned and silently left the bedroom, gently closing the door behind him.

He walked along the hallway towards the stairs, his walk slow – he was shell shocked! Janet had never shown that level of animosity towards him, not once in their forty year marriage. Pausing when he reached the bottom of the stairs, he took a deep breath and tried to digest what had just unfolded. He trudged through to the kitchen, placing his half-empty mug of tea on the worktop and then sat down at the dining table. He had lost his daughter, it seemed he was losing his wife and his entire world was falling apart around him. Overcome with distress, he broke down; deep, painful sobs that hurt his chest. He hadn't cried much since Sara's disappearance, he wanted to remain strong for his wife, and the tears came thick and fast, each harsh intake of breath causing his body to shudder. He was aware, perhaps for the first time, that his life may never be the same again.

CHAPTER 19

Driving down the dirt track that led to the house, the vehicle rocking from side to side on the uneven ground, Michael was focussed. He always ensured he drove carefully down the track, it was imperative if he didn't want to damage his car – it was perilous even for a 4x4! It almost acted like an extra security measure, however, a normal car would never make it down here without attracting attention.

On the passenger seat he had a stack of newspapers and he placed a skeletal hand protectively on top of them to avoid them toppling over as he navigated the treacherous terrain. The newspapers were a mixture of both national and local prints; he had been gathering as many newspapers as he could get his hands on and had accumulated quite the collection. It fascinated him to read about his achievements from the perspective of others and, if he was honest, he quite enjoyed the attention. A wry smile grew across his face as he thought about it.

Pulling up outside the house, he parked in his usual spot and switched off the engine. He leaned over to the passenger seat to gather up his newspapers but halted when he saw raindrops smattering on the windscreen. Placing the newspapers back on the seat, ensuring they weren't going to fall over, he sat back and watched as the weather worsened. He rolled his eyes – he would have to wait now! Rain hadn't been forecast this morning and he hadn't brought an umbrella or any way to protect the newspapers when he took them inside. Patiently, he sat in his vehicle, tapping his long, gangly fingers on the steering wheel. It was so peaceful out here he thought, as he gazed around at the vast woodland. He enjoyed the silence and the isolation of this place, the privacy and security ideal for his current situation. Gazing at his house, his mother's house, he noticed what a state of disrepair it was in. It wasn't something he usually paid much attention to but it wasn't often he sat outside just staring at the building. He pondered over fixing it up a little but he didn't need it to look habitable, he just needed it to be practical and it served that purpose.

As quickly as the rain had arrived, it dispersed and he gathered up his newspapers and made for the house. He trod carefully on the freshly soaked ground, mindful of how slippery it could get and reached the front door without incident. He awkwardly fumbled around for his keys, juggling the pile of newspapers, unlocked the door and entered the property, wiping his feet on the way in.

Once inside, he immediately headed into the living room and placed the mountain of newspapers on an old coffee table. The table was almost entirely covered in a thick layer of dust, except for an area on the main surface which had been previously wiped clean. The room itself didn't contain much furniture and definitely didn't give off the usual homely vibe that a living room would; two musty armchairs faced the coffee table which was centred in the middle of the room, a large antique mirror hung above an unkept fireplace and a considerable portion of the remaining space was taken up by more mounds of newspapers. Michael removed his jacket, carefully folded it and placed it on one of the armchairs before taking a seat in the other.

Picking up a newspaper from the top of the pile, he smiled whilst looking at the front page. It was one of the local newspapers and the headline read 'STILL NOTHING' and was accompanied by a picture of the lead detective, Scott Harris and an article heavily criticising the police department's incompetency. He couldn't get enough of reading that each day; a month later and they still had nothing on him! He laughed out loud, a smug, triumphant laugh and placed the newspaper to one side before picking up another. This one was a national newspaper and, although not front page, it had a multi-page spread on the case so far. He read the article with glee, enjoying the way they described the abduction and the mystery surrounding it. The attention he was getting was thoroughly enjoyable, even with the anonymity.

Having spent so much of his life as a recluse, a ghost, he had grown to crave attention, any attention, just to feel noticed. This situation, however, required secrecy and he would have to enjoy nameless recognition rather than outright fame. He wondered if the media realised what they were doing? By continuously criticising and belittling the police, scrutinising the lack of evidence, highlighting the stagnation of their case, they were merely acknowledging and documenting his genius. He had managed to outthink the whole police force and had made the detectives look useless. He had made a name for himself without his identity being revealed and he felt untouchable. He spent some time flicking through the newspapers, enjoying the representation of his exploits and the description of his successful execution, before placing the newspapers with the abundance of others.

Leaving the living room, he strolled through to the kitchen, his mood overjoyed after his reading time. The kitchen was one of the more well-stocked rooms, although still basic, it had all the necessities required to prepare food and drink. Today was one of his days off work and he had decided to spend all of it with his prize, his love, his 'Little lamb'. She had calmed down considerably since the inception of their unconventional relationship; a development which he could only allude to her finally coming round to his way of thinking, finally seeing how amazing their life together could be. The thought gave him an exuberant rush, his entire plan was coming to fruition exactly the way he had predicted.

It was still early, so he decided he would rustle up some breakfast for Sara. She had been behaving herself and good behaviour deserved a reward. He busied himself frying bacon and eggs on the old hob, placing them in between two slices of toasted bread once completed and added generous lashings of brown sauce. She was going to love this, he just knew it! Filling a mug with instant coffee, he placed it all on a tray and headed out into the hallway, towards the stairs. The standard creak of each step was beginning to grate on his nerves and he decided he would rectify it sometime this week.

Reaching the top of the stairs, he placed the tray on the floor for a moment while he searched in his pockets for the keys. Unlocking the door, he nudged it open, picked up the tray and made his way into the room. He called out in a jovial manner.

'Who wants breakf-' *THWACK!* Something struck him, stinging the side of his head, knocking him to the ground. The tray containing breakfast plummeted to the floor, both the mug and plate shattering on impact, sending coffee, eggs and bacon spewing across the room. He lay on the old floorboards, dazed and shocked as Sara stood over him, clutching a piece of wood, rage plastered across her face. He stared at her, his eyes wide as she drew the piece of wood back a second time and swung it down against his skull, knocking him unconscious.

CHAPTER 20

Waking up, Sara rolled over, stretched and rubbed the sleep from her eyes. She lay still for a moment, staring at the stained ceiling, feeling surprisingly refreshed – she had actually slept pretty well! For the first time, since she was forcibly brought here, she hadn't woken during the night and she felt brand new!

It had been thirty-three days since she got here, she had kept track by scratching a tally into the wall. In that time she had come to understand that the more she complied with her captor, the easier her life became. Her mattress had been upgraded to an actual bed, albeit a tiny single, and he had brought her a small nightlight – she hoped books would be next, something to help pass the time. *He* had even told her his name: Michael. Whether it was his real name or not, she wasn't sure but it had shocked her all the same.

Sitting up, she swung her legs out of the bed and flinched a little when her feet touched down on the cold floor, the sensation making her shudder. Oh, how she *hated* being in this room; it was damp, cold, dirty and lonely. She dragged a bag out from under the bed, reached inside and pulled out a one-size-too-small cardigan which she wrapped around her shoulders to try and combat the cold. Michael had brought her a bag of used women's clothes, probably charity shop finds but they did the job.

After the turbulence of her start as his captive, she had quickly learned that he only reacted badly in extreme circumstances. If she remained calm, so would he. He had become almost caring at times, which unnerved her and he even had a pet name for her: 'Little Lamb.' What the hell was that about? She tried not to contemplate it too much, the answer could be creepier than Michael himself and he really was a creep. When she was in his presence, even when he was being kind, he made her skin crawl. There had been the odd occasion where he had even touched her, nothing too forward but little, almost affectionate acts; a hand on the shoulder, a hand placed on hers. She had resisted every urge to pull away in disgust in those instances, her aim was to gain his trust… to survive.

She worried that she would never be found here, the location was so remote and her fears had been confirmed when Michael had shown her a newspaper – the police had nothing. He was almost smug when he had shown her, an obvious show of control. The knowledge that they were struggling to find her had scared her but it had also kicked her into survival mode. She just hoped she could keep up this facade long enough for him to slip up, to make a mistake.

Her thoughts were interrupted by the recognisable rumble of his 4x4 along the dirt track and her stomach sank. He was here early today, which meant he wasn't working, which meant she had to playact all day. Getting up, she approached the window and watched as his vehicle pulled up in the usual spot. She could see the usual collection of newspapers on the passenger seat, he seemed to thoroughly enjoy reading about the ongoing case. Droplets of rain began to appear on the window pane and Sara watched as Michael sat in his car, avoiding the sudden downpour. His reluctance to get himself or his precious newspapers wet gave her time to get into her persona; to mentally prepare herself to feign benevolence.

The precipitation began to ease and once it had cleared, Michael gathered his newspapers, vacated his vehicle and headed towards the house. Sara turned away from the window and as she did so, she caught her bare foot on a loose nail that was sticking up from one of the dilapidated floorboards. She cursed as she clutched her foot, blood gushing from the fresh wound on the outside of her appendage. While she continued to utter profanities and attempt to stem the bleeding, the floorboard that had caused her injury caught her eye. The entire end was protruding from its original position, both nails loose. Forgetting about the small laceration, she slid across the dusty floor for a closer inspection. Gingerly, she felt around the raised edge and managed to prise it up further. Creating a gap, she squeezed her fingers into the space and began to pull. The old, wooden plank began to crack and splinter under the pressure she was applying and she increased her force. With one last effort the wood made a rewarding tearing sound as it ripped free from where it was attached.

Sara, on her knees, cradelled the old piece of wood; it may have been a little battered but it was still heavy, still solid enough. She remained quiet for a moment, listening to Michael pottering around downstairs, ensuring that he hadn't heard her wrench the piece of timber free. Was this her chance? Could she use this as a weapon? Just bide her time, wait for him to come upstairs…

The scent of bacon was wafting up from the kitchen, drifting into her nostrils. A scent that would have left her mouth watering a month ago, now made her apprehensive. It meant he would be coming upstairs with breakfast soon and she had very little time to make a decision. Did she risk it? If it paid off she could be free. If it went sideways how would he react? Would it finally push him over the edge? If she didn't go through with it, how the bloody hell would she explain the floorboard she had ripped up?

She heard his footsteps on the stairs, the familiar sound of the creaky floorboards acting like a countdown, forcing her to make a decision. She stood up and positioned herself to the side of the door, her heart was thumping, adrenaline surging through her body. Was she really going to attempt this? The creaking ceased, heralding the end of his ascent. Clutching the plank, her knuckles turning white, she raised it above her head. She listened intently as he fumbled around with the keys, her mouth dry and her nervousness increasing. The door swung open and he entered carrying a tray, without hesitation she brought the plank of wood down on the side of his head with a satisfying thud. Michael fell to the floor, the tray going with him, food and coffee going everywhere and the dinnerware smashing to pieces. Looking down at him, Sara could see the shock on his face and she raised the piece of wood a second time. Putting all of her strength into this swing it connected accurately with his head, the sound sickening as it broke through the skin and he was out cold. Sara dropped the improvised weapon to the floor, her chest heaving with her heavy, panicked breaths. She stared down at him, blood gushing from the split in his head that she had caused, feeling a little sick.

Seizing her opportunity, she stepped over his limp, lifeless body and bolted down the stairs. Knowing she wouldn't have long, she was rushing and reached the front door swiftly – it was locked. Yanking at it furiously, she hoped it would open but she had no luck. He had the keys on him, why didn't she think to grab them? Idiot! But it was too late, she couldn't go back upstairs now, it was too risky – what if he woke up? She just had to find a way out quickly.

Growing frantic she ran into the living room and tried the window, it was sealed shut just like the one in her bedroom. She was beginning to feel faint, her breathing getting increasingly erratic from the panic. Running through to the kitchen, she tried the window in there, sealed as well! She knew she was running out of time, there had to be a way out, it wasn't Fort Knox! Rushing back out into the hallway, she sprinted past the stairs towards the back of the house and opened a door into an old utility room. Her eyes scanned the room quickly, there was a large amount of natural light coming from a small hallway on the other side of the room. Running toward the origin of the light, she was relieved to find a back door. She tried opening it first, locked of course, but it was a two panel glass door – she just needed something to smash it! She turned back into the utility and grabbed a small wooden stool that she had passed on her way in. Taking it to the back door, she swung it with all her strength at the top pane. It shattered into large shards and she used the stool to clear any remaining pieces so she could climb through without cutting herself.

Throwing the stool to the floor, she began to clamber through the now glassless opening, her right leg first. She was still barefoot so she was cautious as she tentatively placed her foot in between the shards of glass. She could feel the fresh air on her face and welcomed it, she was so close to freedom. She steadied herself, holding on to the door frame and as she began to lift her left leg up and over, she felt herself being jerked backwards.

She hit the deck with a thud, Michael had got to her and pulled her backwards by her hair. Looking up at him, his blood-covered face was contorted with fury, he looked terrifying. He bent down and grabbed her hair again and began dragging her from the room. The heavy landing had winded her and she weakly kicked and screamed, grabbing at his hands to try and free herself from his grasp. He was showing a level of strength she hadn't witnessed before as he dragged her along the hallway and up the stairs, her back bashing painfully on the edge of each step.

Reaching the room, *her* room, he pulled her up by her hair so her face was level with his.

'You stupid, STUPID, little girl!' He threw her roughly to the ground and she watched, fear stricken as he approached her, his fists clenched.

'Acts of impulse like that cannot go unpunished – you will regret that decision!'

She closed her eyes tightly and prayed that, whatever he was about to do, he did it quickly.

CHAPTER 21

April 2017

Standing up from his desk with such ferocity that his chair shot back and tipped over, Scott couldn't believe what he had just heard. With his phone firmly pressed against his ear, he listened avidly as an officer from the next county over said the words he had been waiting to hear for months – there had been a potential sighting of Sara Williams.

Hastily scribbling down the location, he slammed the phone back down on the receiver and stood for a moment, shellshocked. His breathing was shallow and rapid, excitement coursing through his body causing a tingling sensation in his hands and feet. Months… months he had been working himself to the point of exhaustion and they could finally have a breakthrough.

Several pairs of eyes were staring him down and he snapped out of his adrenaline induced stupor, gathered his things and vacated his workspace. Marching away from his desk, his pace was brisk and his walk full of intent. This was a man on a mission, a man who could see the light at the end of the tunnel. He got to the break room, where he knew Detective Constable Lock was. As he entered, Lock looked up from where he was sitting, a single, solitary bite taken from the sandwich that was clutched in his hands.

'Possible sighting of Sara Williams, we have to go.... now!' Scott turned on a sixpence and strode away. Lock discarded his sandwich and swiftly joined Detective Harris.

'Where has she been seen, Sarge?' Lock inquired.

'A little over an hour away at a motorway services, so we need to get going right now.' Scott was breathless. 'Can you make a call and get some of our uniforms to meet us there, bodies that are familiar with the case? The station that got the call has already sent out patrol cars to try and track down the vehicle she was seen in. They said the manager who called was almost one hundred percent certain it was her. This could be it, mate!' His voice was almost jovial.

Lock didn't respond vocally, he just got on his phone and made the call. By the time they had reached Scott's vehicle, everything was in motion and they were on their way.

Arriving at the services, located next to a busy motorway, Scott was pleased to see multiple uniformed officers already talking to members of the public. He vacated his vehicle, with Lock joining him and made their way to the entrance of the services, quickly flashing their badges to the officer who stood guard at the door as they walked inside.

The two detectives strode toward the front desk, Scott a little ahead of Lock, a slight grin spread across his tired, unshaven face. He knew nothing was certain but he couldn't suppress his optimism, this could end up being the lead they had been waiting for, finally a potential sighting. If it ended up panning out, they knew they were closing in on the perpetrator and hopefully the opportunity to find Sara alive.

Approaching the front desk, where the checkouts were situated, Scott immediately engaged the manager – the woman who had called this in.

'Hi, I'm Detective Sergeant Scott Harris, this is Detective Constable James Lock' Scott gestured towards his colleague and they presented their badges in unison. 'You're the one who called this in?' Scott clarified and was met with an almost nervous nod. 'You have CCTV footage?' She nodded again. 'We need to see it, please.'

Wordlessly the manager motioned them to follow and led them through to the back of the store. Reaching a small office, she unlocked the door and entered with the two detectives following. She took her place at a seat in front of a computer with the detectives standing on either side of her. Clicking 'play' on a pre-recorded video, from behind the front desk, they were looking at a caucasian male, roughly in his forties.

'This was the man who owned the vehicle we saw the girl in' the manager told them. 'This is the girl' she said, clicking play on another video. This footage was from a camera that was pointing at the pump that the car had been parked at. The image wasn't as clear as the previous one and both detectives leaned in close to inspect the girl in the car. Examining her face, Scott celebrated internally – it looked just like her! It looked as though they had finally found her.

Standing up straight he looked at Lock and they shared a smile, it seemed they were in agreement – it was Sara! They vacated the security office and walked back through the service station, their spirits lifted now they actually had a lead but as they walked outside on to the forecourt, Scott's phone rang. Answering promptly, he listened to the voice on the other end of the line. Lock watched as Scott listened without responding and saw his previously elated expression turn to one of anger and disappointment. Hanging up, he clenched his phone tightly in his hand, turned around and threw it to the floor – the mobile shattering on impact. Sinking to his knees, his head in his hands, the elation from just seconds earlier was gone.

'They located the car, it wasn't her, Lock. It wasn't her.'

* * *

Several days after the disappointment of the mistaken sighting, Scott was sitting at his desk wracking his mind on what direction to go in next. The problem was they had nothing to use, nothing to go on and they were relying heavily on the public for a sighting or breakthrough.

He sighed, still feeling a little deflated and rubbed harshly at his tired eyes. Glancing up, his eyes adjusting to the light he saw Superintendent Wilson gesturing to him, signifying he wanted to see him in his office. Scott nodded to acknowledge the summoning and then made his way there.

Entering, he closed the door behind him and immediately took a seat opposite his superior. Nick began speaking immediately.

'Sergeant, we are pulling some of the resources from the Sara Williams case. You will still be leading the investigation but with a much smaller team. Detective Constable Lock will no longer be aiding you, I need him to investigate some other cases. We just can't afford to have this many personnel on a case when no progress is being made. I'm sure you understand?' The question was rhetorical.

Scott sat for a moment, silent and defeated, before nodding curtly and leaving Nick's office. This had been a bloody awful week, an awful few months, in fact. Now he had to deliver more news, more bad news to The Williams and be the one to tell them that the search for their missing daughter was being scaled down. If a hole suddenly opened up in front of him and swallowed him, it wouldn't be a bad thing.

CHAPTER 22

Gently closing the front door, Janet Williams welcomed the relief she felt as the detective left her home. As much as she appreciated his efforts, he had recently become the exclusive bearer of bad news. It was only a few days earlier he had been there to reveal that the reported sighting of her daughter had been a dead end, a case of mistaken identity. The rush of euphoric optimism she had felt that day had been a welcome feeling but she had been brought crashing down to earth with an incredibly painful bump. Today, he had arrived with the news that resources were being cut from the investigation into the disappearance of her only child. As much as she understood the reasons why, deep down, she still resented the police force for what she saw as abandoning her daughter.

Janet had been a mess for the last few months, the disappearance of Sara, her little miracle baby, had left her a broken woman. Eventually she had found a way to function, a way to exist without her baby but she wasn't the same person as she was several months prior.

Peter, her husband, had been brilliant. He'd been helpful and caring, attentive and considerate, all whilst dealing with his own anguish. Janet, on the other hand, had been incredibly selfish, and she was aware of the fact, but she had lost her ability to feel empathy. All she cared about, all she wanted, was to get her daughter back. The problem she was having was that with each passing day, with each fresh bout of bad news, she felt as though the likelihood of her daughter being returned to her was becoming increasingly doubtful.

Walking through the immaculate hallway of their home, she made a beeline for the kitchen where her husband was beginning to wash the mugs from the tea they had during the visit from the detective. She watched him for a moment while he filled the sink with water, just drinking him in. He was still a handsome man, tall and broad with silver hair that complimented his olive skin tone. Oh, how she adored him, she just wished she had in her to show him how much. He really had been incredible throughout this whole ordeal, suffering in silence while she was being difficult and self-centred.

'Love, I think I'm going to have a hot bath, I need to unwind a little.'

Peter turned to face her and she could see he had been crying – this latest news obviously affecting him a huge amount.

'OK, my dear' he responded. 'Do you need me to bring you anything?'

Janet knew she should've stayed and consoled her husband but instead, she politely declined his offer and just made her way upstairs to the bathroom. Closing and locking the door behind her, she turned on the taps and then poured a generous amount of bubble bath into the rapidly rising water. The soothing smell of lavender began to permeate around the room as the steam rose from the hot liquid and she could feel the tension in her body disappearing.

Walking over to the medicine cabinet, she opened it and grabbed the anti-depressants she had relied on for the last few months. They by no means made her happy but they did help to just calm her down a little and decrease her anxiety. Opening the pot, she reached into it with a finger and dragged out two pills before popping them without water. Placing the lid back on the pot, she placed it on the edge of the bath, rather than returning it to the cabinet, and began to undress.

For her age, Janet was still an attractive woman; long, thick, dyed-blonde hair tumbled past her shoulders, her eyes were a deep jade, the same as her daughter's and were framed with an abundance of crow's feet. Her lips, vermillion and full, were pursed over a set of brilliant white teeth. She exercised often, practised yoga and ate healthy, wholesome food.

Staring at her body in the mirror, she knew she could still turn heads, even from the younger men but the fact meant nothing to her anymore, there wasn't a lot she truly cared about these days.

With the bath brimmed, she turned off the taps, checked that it was a comfortable temperature and slowly slipped into the water. She savoured the warm sensation that enveloped her as she submerged herself and relaxed. Suddenly, the tears came, thick and fast. This happened a lot, it was hard to control the emotions that she constantly attempted to stifle. Reaching over to the pot of pills, she opened it and threw another two tablets into her mouth, swallowing them uncomfortably before returning them to their position on the side of the bath. The crying increased as the last few days finally took their toll on her, defeating her resolve. The sobbing was loud and painful, each deep gasp for breath in between cries making her chest ache.

The fact that the police were scaling back their efforts could only mean one thing in her mind and that was that they didn't think her daughter was going to be found. Before today, she hadn't allowed herself to think that there was no hope that she would see her daughter again. Her *only* daughter, her only child, and her best friend was gone.

Still weeping uncontrollably, she reached out for her remaining antidepressants and swallowed what was left before discarding the empty container on the floor. She didn't want to live like this anymore, she didn't want to wake up each day distraught and falling apart – she just wanted this pain to end. Several minutes passed and her crying continued, during that period her heart rate had increased dramatically and she was beginning to feel nauseous – the drugs were beginning to take effect. She began to shake as more time passed and eventually slipped into unconsciousness, her body going limp and as it did so, she slid down in the bath, her head disappearing beneath the bubbles.

CHAPTER 23

Placing the freshly washed tea mugs in the cupboard, Peter chucked the damp tea towel on the kitchen worktop and collapsed into a seat at the dining table. Today's news had knocked him for six and he felt exhausted, defeated and lost. His wife, once again, had seen him struggling and continued her trend of not caring an ounce. Not only did it hurt him deeply, that she couldn't just find it in herself to realise that this was hard for him too, but it left him frustrated and irritated. Up to this point he had put up with it, he had dealt with his own sadness alone, all the while ensuring he was there for her, but he had finally reached breaking point.

Deep down, he'd had enough of the selfishness for a while but it was finally rising to the surface. He'd had enough of feeling alone, feeling unsupported and being his wife's emotional punching bag. These last few months, he had suffered alone, dealt with his turmoil internally without any comfort from the woman he married and he was beginning to resent her for it.

Standing up, he paced the kitchen trying to suppress the rage that was building inside of him. His daughter was missing and it seemed like the chances of finding her were increasingly unlikely, he also felt as though he was losing his wife. The kind, thoughtful, wonderful woman he had married was long gone, replaced by a selfish, difficult woman who he was beginning to abhor being in the presence of.

The anger and frustration he was feeling was bubbling away inside of him, a hot ball of fury that was growing in the pit of his stomach. This couldn't go on, this one-sided, unsupportive arrangement could not continue, for both their sakes. Sara was his daughter as well and they needed to be there for each other, it was the only way they would be able to survive this. It was about time he articulated this to Janet, he had let this go on for too long, just trying to be understanding but this atrocious week had pushed him over the edge.

Marching from the kitchen, he made for the stairs. With his wife in the bath, she wouldn't be able to escape the conversion and they could hopefully find a solution. It was time he got this off his chest, he *needed* to get this off his chest.

Reaching the bathroom door he turned the door knob and was met with resistance as he went to push it open – it was locked. Knocking on the door, he called out to his wife, his tone gentle and his voice quivering. Silence. 'Janet?' he called out again and was greeted with silence once more. Panicking a little, he rapped at the door loudly and yelled out to his wife. 'JANET! TALK TO ME!' Nothing. The silence sent a chill down his spine, something wasn't right.

Shuffling back he picked his spot and threw all his weight forward into the door, his shoulder connecting with the wood with a loud thud but the door held firm. Retreating further he launched himself forward with all his might and the door flew open, the splintering of the wood resounding against the quietness of the house as it ripped from the frame.

The sight he was met with made his heart stop: his wife was fully submerged in the bath water, unmoving. An empty pill pot was discarded on the bathroom floor. Lunging forward he grabbed her lifeless body and frantically dragged her from the bath and onto the floor, beginning CPR without hesitation. After the first lot of compressions, he pulled his phone from his pocket, dialled '999' and threw the phone on the floor on speakerphone, before continuing compressions.

'Emergency. Which service?' the operator asked.

'Paramedics!' he yelled. 'My wife isn't breathing, I think she overdosed, please be quick!' He was breathing heavily from the compressions but just about managed to call out his address.

After what seemed like an eternity, but in reality was just a few minutes, paramedics had burst into the house and had taken over from him. He watched on helplessly as the paramedics set about trying to save his wife. Slumping to the floor, his head in his hands, the tears began to gently roll down his flushed cheeks. Was this really happening? Was he about to lose his wife as well?

Just as he thought the worst case scenario was unfolding, his wife spluttered awake, rolled onto her side and vomited across the bathroom floor. One of the paramedics was immediately on their phone, making arrangements for the hospital to be ready for her arrival. She wasn't out of the woods just yet but Peter was just grateful to see her breathing. Leaning forward, he grabbed her hand and held it tight, relieved and grateful that the love of his life was still with him.

CHAPTER 24

October 2017

Laying awake staring into the empty darkness, DS Scott Harris sighed loudly. It was three a.m. and, once again, unwanted consciousness had bested much needed sleep. Another restless, disturbed night to add to many others. It had been some time since Scott had slept properly and he was beyond exhausted.

He had been working the case of Sara Williams' disappearance for almost a year, a year in which they had come up with absolutely nothing. There hadn't been a single concrete development in that entire time, something Scott wasn't accustomed to – he had never had a case open for this long. In that time period, they had two reported sightings of Sara, which both ended up being false. Those moments of excitement and hopefulness had been quickly replaced by disappointment and deflation.

As the months went on, the pressure on him increased, the stress became almost unbearable and the department had ended up pulling some of his resources.

They couldn't rationalise the amount of manpower they were utilising, only to have no results. DC Lock had been reassigned to other cases and Scott had continued to pursue answers with a much smaller and less experienced team. It had become clear that his superiors had decided this case was becoming a lost cause, something Scott could never agree with – how could a human life be a lost cause? Giving up just wasn't an option for him.

Things had gotten worse when the news broke that they were reducing their efforts. They had alerted the parents before making it public knowledge and Janet Williams had attempted to take her own life, news that had come as a sucker punch to Scott. Janet had suffered immensely after Sara went missing and had struggled to come to terms with it, her mental health steadily deteriorating as the months passed. When she had received the news that they were downscaling the resources on the case, she had attempted an overdose. Her husband, Sara's father Pete, had found her unconscious and unresponsive and called paramedics immediately. Fortunately, they had managed to save her life and she had been on the road to recovery ever since, finally getting adequate help and support.

The whole incident had affected Scott severely, he still blamed himself for the fact that they hadn't been able to find Sara and, in turn, felt wholly responsible for the family's turmoil. The guilt had been overwhelming but he had to put his own feelings aside and persevere with the case, he could still make this right! However, several months had passed and they were still no closer to a breakthrough and the case had consumed him. Whatever life he had before Sara's disappearance was now non-existent.

Time trickled away while he lay awake pondering his next move and his six forty-five a.m. alarm was soon chiming into his thoughts, signalling the inception of what was likely to be another disheartening day of detective work.

Sitting up, he flicked on his bedside lamp and the artificial light filled his bedroom. Casting an eye across the room, he was fully aware of the chaos he had become attuned to living in. Scott had never been a particularly tidy person but he had taken his slovenliness to a whole new level. Old, crinkled suits and shirts littered the bedroom floor, worn ties thrown randomly on multiple surfaces and the doors of the wardrobe were wide open, displaying the scant amount of clean outfits he had remaining.

Unsteadily and tiredly, he got up out of bed and navigated his way through the detritus that lay strewn on the floor. As always, he headed straight through to his bathroom to empty his bladder and then brush his teeth. Standing in front of the mirror he surveyed the way he looked, disgusted with himself. Scott was a shadow of his former self; his weight had plummeted and a once sturdy, muscular physique had been replaced with a frail, scrawny figure. His facial hair had grown scraggly and unkempt, his dark hair, that once worked for him effortlessly, looked thinner and dry; he knew he looked like death warmed up but he long dropped any concerns over his appearance, there were more pressing matters to spend his time on.

Ambling back to his bedroom, he approached his open wardrobe to select a suit for the day. Choice was beginning to dwindle, he really needed to find time to make a trip to the dry cleaners. Selecting a stylish grey suit from his limited selection, he matched it with a pale blue shirt and navy blue tie. The suit, which would've once complimented his frame, hung loose and accentuated his drastic weight loss. He rummaged around the floor amongst the disarray, finding a pair of unwashed black socks and sniffed them, deciding that they would suffice. Once his outfit was complete, he grabbed his mobile phone and lumbered downstairs.

Scott walked into his kitchen, another room that was an absolute shambles; there were more dirty cups and dishes than there were clean and the scent of old food from the brimmed rubbish bin was on assault on his nostrils. He grimaced as he got a whiff of it and quickly opened the back door for fresh air. A gentle, misty rain was falling and he decided against stepping outside for a cigarette, instead opting to stand at the threshold and blow the cigarette out into the autumn air. Drawing in a lungful of smoke, he relished the hit of nicotine before releasing a cloud of smoke that drifted lazily in front of his face, gradually dispersing. Several drags later, he had finished the cigarette and casually flicked the butt into a puddle before closing the back door. He turned and checked that the kettle had enough water in before turning it on and opening a cupboard to grab a mug. Swinging the cupboard door open, he was greeted with an empty space, unsurprising given the mountain of unwashed dishes in the sink. Not bothering to wash a mug, he decided he would grab a coffee on his way to work. Leaving the kitchen, the kettle still boiling away, he strolled out into the hallway, put on a pair of scuffed black shoes, grabbed his coat, his car keys, and headed out into the morning air.

Pulling into his usual spot at the station a little early, he could already feel the onset of trepidation. Work doesn't have the same level of satisfaction when you're unable to produce results. He sipped at the coffee he had purchased en route, the to-go cup saturated with condensation on its exterior. The warmth of the liquid was satisfying and he savoured these few moments of calm before another day in the proverbial line of fire. The issue he was having today, was he actually had no plan of which direction to go in next, he was at a loss. No leads, no new evidence, nothing of note for him to work with – he needed to conjure something out of thin air! He was failing and he didn't like the way it made him feel. For the first time in his career he was receiving more criticism than plaudits and that was a tough pill to swallow.

Vacating his car and stepping out into the brisk, moisture-laden air, he immediately lit a cigarette. The gentle breeze was cold and refreshing and he welcomed the invigorating feeling. He approached the station entrance slowly, enjoying his second cigarette of the day and the brief moment of quiet and tranquillity before another taxing day. He disposed of his cigarette when he reached the steps that led to the station entrance and entered the building.

He walked through the foyer and down the corridor with purpose, unwilling to engage with anyone he passed, as usual. Getting to the large doors that led to his domain, he punched the code in the keypad and swiftly headed to the conference room where he had spent the last eleven months. There was no one else in the room when he arrived, just the same boxes of evidence and files that had been gathered. It all seemed a little illusional now, not a single thing had led to a significant breakthrough.

Taking his place in his usual seat, he sat for a moment, trying to produce a new approach to this case from the depths of his mind. They had exhausted most channels and he was running out of options; without something new to go on they really were clutching at straws. He had been given a couple of new detectives to help him continue this case, when they had reduced his resources, and he decided he would get them back out and about where Sara was taken. It wasn't uncommon for criminals to return to the scene of their crimes, it was good to remain vigilant and keep an eye out for any odd behaviour. Satisfied with his approach, for today at least, he decided he would take another look at the photos from the woodland where they were certain Sara was taken through – Scott liked to remain familiar with the site. Taking the file of photos out from one of the evidence boxes, he placed them on the table in front of him and began scanning them. Suddenly a voice interrupted his focus.

'Oh good, you're here.' It was Nick's secretary. 'The superintendent would like to see you, Sergeant.' She waited for Scott's acknowledgement, which came in the form of a curt nod, and turned and left. Scott packed the photos back in the box and strolled down to Nick's office, another dressing down heading his way no doubt.

He knocked and opened the door simultaneously, not waiting for instruction to enter. Nick was sitting behind his desk, his hands resting on the surface with his fingers laced, a serious expression on his face.

'Morning Boss' Scott greeted his superior.

The greeting wasn't returned, Nick just motioned towards a vacant chair. 'Please have a seat, Sergeant.'

Scott sat down, aware that there was a tangible tension in the room, an atmosphere between the two of them. He had a sinking feeling in his stomach and felt as though he was about to be told something he didn't want to hear. Across the desk Nick sat very still, his expression unchanging. Clearing his throat loudly, he got straight to the point.

'We're pulling all resources from the abduction case, Scott.' Nick paused, allowing the statement to sink in. Scott didn't react and Nick continued.

'It's gone cold, Scott, and we can't continue to waste time and money. We haven't had a new lead for months and everything we had prior was a dead end. The case will remain open, as will the public hotlines and if any new evidence comes up, you'll be the first to know. I'll need you to pack up everything in the conference room as well, please. I'll be letting the parents know this morning and we'll be holding a televised press conference this afternoon.'

Scott sat, unblinking and silent, causing Nick to shift uncomfortably in his seat. Scott couldn't believe what he was hearing, his heart was in his throat and he could feel his pulse quickening. He clenched his fists tightly, stifling the sudden rage inside him. They were giving up on her? That was it? No closure for the parents, no closure for him… and what about Janet? She had already tried ending her life once during all this, how was she going to take this?

He stared at his superior, choking down the angry outburst that was on the tip of his tongue and responded 'Understood' before getting up from his seat and leaving Nick's office.

Wandering back to the conference room, he felt dazed – he couldn't believe it. Sara could be somewhere waiting and hoping for them to find her and they were just giving up? Like she was *nothing?* The mixture of confusion and anger was making him feel sick.

Entering the conference room, he looked around at the scarce amount of evidence. It was pathetic, it was pitiful… He had failed and it had probably cost Sara her life. The emotion was too much to bear and he let out a frustrated roar as he flipped the table with the evidence boxes on. The table crashed to the ground, the boxes bursting open sending files and paperwork everywhere. Colleagues of his had stopped what they were doing and were watching through the window as he unleashed. He completely trashed the room; tearing down the whiteboards, flipping the remaining tables and throwing chairs.

His anger subsided and, his energy spent, he leant against the wall and slumped down to the floor, burying his head in his hands. With his gaze directed at the floor, something caught his eye – it was Sara's earring. It had been found the first morning they were looking around the park and was now safely nestled in an evidence bag. Picking it up, he clutched it tightly to his chest and the tears began to flow.

CHAPTER 25

Strolling through the remote woodland, Michael Thompson felt at peace. The soothing solitude of his walks in the forest were medicinal for him, taking him away from the stresses and pressure of his double life. He had grown to appreciate these moments of 'me time' and found them to be incredibly therapeutic.

A light, misty rain was falling around him, gradually covering him in a blanket of moisture. Gentle gusts of wind were making the pine trees sway, occasionally forcing pinecones from the safety of their perches, dropping them to the ground with a gentle thud. The roots of the trees were working hard to keep them stable against the breeze, gentle groans from the creaking wood amplified against the silence. Occasional shrieks and squawks from the native birds piercing the eerie quietude. These lonely walks had become a bi-daily ritual for Michael and he savoured every step on the soft ground.

It had been a tough, tiring year – he had worked very hard to maintain his secret. Living two separate lives was exhausting and ensuring anonymity whilst simultaneously craving attention was a mental conflict he found troubling. He had managed to keep his urges under control, however, and enjoyed his nameless infamy from afar. It had been a development he hadn't expected when he took Sara but hearing and reading about himself had become addictive. There had been several occasions, since his first encounter with DS Scott Harris, where he had wanted to get close to the investigation – the rush he had felt that one time was exhilarating! Common sense had prevailed, though, and he battled his urges and avoided taking risks – there was no need to draw significant attention to himself. Getting away with a crime had been much easier than he envisioned, why ruin it?

Life had fallen into place for him since he had taken his 'Little Lamb'. The beginning had been difficult and he and Sara had clashed several times, like all relationships really, but her behaviour had improved and eventually she had calmed down. He was beyond grateful for her change in mindset, it meant he could relax a little and not worry about getting attacked any time he entered her bedroom. He had even done his best to consolidate these positive changes and reward her good behaviour by furnishing her bedroom a little more. If he could make her feel at home, she might start treating it like one.

Michael still had his job at the newsagents and still had his little flat, it was vital that he kept these things in place, live a normal life and just fade into the background as he always had. No one around him knew that he was anything other than a quiet recluse and that was ideal, it allowed him to live this second life undisturbed.

He still enjoyed following the news, hearing them talk about him without having a clue who he was – they were all so stupid! It was gratifying to know how much smarter he was, how he could pull this off and sit back and watch while they turned him into a celebrity, he smiled at the thought. Despite the fact that the case wasn't as well covered as eleven months prior, he still watched the news daily just in case – it was something to look forward to. The thought of the news snapped him out of his daydream and he checked his watch, he would have to get back soon if he didn't want to miss today's evening news.

The sun was setting and twilight was descending over the woodland. Deciding to head back, he spun around and began his journey back to the house – being alone in the woodland when darkness fell wasn't something he was keen on. His walk was hurried as he tried to beat the ever increasing darkness, the temperature dropping and each breath showed as a plume of white steam that trailed behind him.

By the time he had reached his house, darkness had almost completely replaced light and the moon shone down on him like a celestial guardian; the rain had stopped and the cool evening air made him shiver. Kicking the mud of his boots, he took them off outside before heading through the front door and into the house. Glancing up the stairs, he could see light creeping out from under Sara's bedroom door and it made him smile, he would go up and see her in a little while.

Wandering through to the living room, he switched on a lamp and then turned on the TV he had bought a few months prior – watching the news on his iPad had become tedious. He had timed his return to perfection and had a few minutes to spare before the news started. He may not hear about himself as much these days but the possibility still excited him; fame was a fickle beast and it came in waves. Making himself comfortable, he sat back and listened to the familiar theme music that signified the beginning of the news and awaited the headlines. The newscaster appeared on screen; 'Coming up… updates on the disappearance of Sara Williams, a live press conference from the investigating officers. We also take a look at…'

Her voice trailed off as Michael stopped listening and he sat, flabbergasted. A live press conference?

Where did this come from? They hadn't done one for ages! Had they found something? His heart was hammering inside his rib cage, his palms sweating profusely; the feeling of nervousness and apprehension was so tangible he could taste it. Could this be the beginning of the end for him? He would have to wait, find out and react accordingly.

Growing impatient, he watched the other news stories with bated breath while waiting for the press conference. He was staring at the screen but he wasn't listening, he was lost in his own mind. 'They must have had a breakthrough' he thought out loud, why else would they be publicising this announcement so heavily? Just as everything had fallen into place, they were going to tear it apart. The newscaster's voice interrupted his panicked thoughts; 'Now we go live to the police press conference, warning there may be flash photography throughout.'

Michael sat forward waiting and listening intently as the camera cut to the recognisable room where they had held every press gathering. The table, empty at the moment, had two seats and two microphones prepared; he could hear the indistinct chatter of the assembled press as they awaited this surprise announcement. Michael watched as Superintendent Nick Wilson came into shot and took a seat, alone. The chatter died down, replaced by the sound of camera shutters clicking away and flashbulbs going off repeatedly. The seat next to Nick remained vacant as he began to read from a prepared statement.

'Thank you all for coming here today on short notice. We have asked you all here so we can give you an update on the case of the abduction of Sara Williams.' He paused for a moment, glanced at the empty seat next to him and continued. 'We have come to the very difficult decision to pull our investigative resources from the case. This isn't an eventuality we have come to lightly and it is with a heavy heart that we have to do this. All probative investigative leads were exhausted months ago and we have had nothing new since then. Unfortunately, we can't rationalise the amount of time and money we are spending on a case that isn't making any progress. I would like to make it abundantly clear that we are not closing this case and our hotline will remain open – the number will be on your screens at home and is on the board behind me. If you think you have anything that can help us find Sara, please don't hesitate to call. I have personally spoken with Mr and Mrs Williams and we have officers supporting them at this difficult time. Once again, thank you for coming here today, I won't be taking any questions.' With that, Nick stood up and walked out of shot, cameras going off wildly and journalists yelling out questions that would remain unanswered.

The screen cut back to the newscaster and Michael switched off the television before sitting back in his chair and taking a long, deep breath. They had nothing! He had done it, that was it, it was over! She was all his now, they had practically given her to him! He deserved her if that's how much they care about her! They had just given up on her! They had just given up on *him!* His relief was quickly replaced by confusion and anger, this meant he would no longer be talked about! Once again, he would fade away, eventually becoming a distant memory. The swell of anger and frustration surged through his body, how dare they act as if he was *nothing!*

He began pacing around the living room, upset that they were snatching his fame away from him. It was never something he had planned but he had finally been noticed, he had been someone! Enraged, he walked over to the television, picked it up and slammed it through the coffee table; shards of wood and plastic erupted across the room. His usual calm demeanour had been replaced by one of pure, unadulterated fury. Picking up his newspapers, his souvenirs, he began ripping at them, tearing them to shreds and throwing the remnants all over the place before unleashing a hellish bellow. His whole life he had been worthless, he had been a ghost and he had enjoyed people finally being aware of his existence, even if it was without his identity being known.

Marching from the living room, he stomped up the stairs; seeing his 'Little Lamb' was the only thing that could assuage him right now. It was just the two of them now and that was all he had ever really wanted.

CHAPTER 26

Looking out from her bedroom window, Sara was transfixed by the gentle swaying of the pine trees in the wind. It was mesmerising as the gusts rocked them from side to side like a boat on choppy waters. A light, misty rain was falling and droplets of water raced down the outside of the window pane; the weather looked miserable and gloomy but in her room, she felt warm and cosy.

Turning away from the window, she glanced around her bedroom, much changed since her first night in captivity. A space that was once dirty, dank and desolate was now homely and inviting. Gradually throughout her time here, he had allowed her to make the dwelling more comfortable, more hospitable. After her unsuccessful escape attempt almost a year prior, she had finally accepted that compliance was what would keep her alive; the only time she had ever felt threatened was when she had challenged him. Since that realisation she hadn't stepped out of line, hadn't argued, hadn't even pondered a new escape plan. She even engaged him in conversation, something he really seemed to relish. He was a strange character, very eccentric but he was also predictable, a creature of habit. Paying attention to his actions and learning his personality traits was something that had made her life in confinement much more bearable.

His violent flashes had only been in response to her defiance and the conflict always seemed to deeply upset him. It was clearly a situation they both wanted to avoid and, by indulging him a little, her new existence had become much less threatening. This approach had paid off, there had been no violence or aggressive behaviour and he had actually rewarded her with things that gradually turned her prison into a home.

In the corner of the room, where once her lonely mattress had been, now stood an actual bed. The difference the bed had made to her inconsistent sleep routine had been astronomical and helped give her the energy to keep up her charade. Next to the bed was a small bedside table, with a lamp on top of it; along the same wall was a bookshelf, safely stowing the reading material he had brought her to keep her occupied. Against the opposite wall, a wardrobe stood solitary, holding a small selection of clothes that he had gotten her. In one of the other corners of the room, an electric heater whirred away, circulating warm air, creating a snug and pleasant environment. The floor, which had once been covered in a thick layer of dust, had been swept and cleaned, the floorboard she had ripped up to use as a weapon had been replaced and a thick, fluffy rug completed the look. A home away from home, making the best of a very bad situation.

She had managed to cultivate an easier way to cope with this ordeal through learning patience. She would be found eventually, if he had planned on killing her she would've been in a shallow grave by now, she just had to wait it out and try and make her time as easy as possible. She allowed herself a little chuckle as she realised her thought process was much like that of a newly incarcerated criminal.

The sound of Michael getting home from one of his walks interrupted her thoughts and she heard him enter the house. His return didn't herald the same fear and panic it once had, he was actually incredibly docile unless challenged with resistance. She listened as the gentle sounds of the television drifted upstairs – he would be watching the news as always. It had initially disturbed her how enthusiastic he was to watch the news, purely to hear them talk about his own crime. However, she had come to look forward to him relaying the information, the updates were her only connection to the outside world. He would be up to see her after the news, like clockwork so she grabbed a book and settled down on the bed to occupy herself before his arrival.

Relaxing, she idly flicked through one of her pieces of literature but not really absorbing the content, she was just passing time before he came upstairs with his daily news update and dinner – her stomach was beginning to rumble aggressively. It was odd, at that moment, she actually felt quite content, something she never thought she would be able to feel while being held against her will. It was surprising how resolute the human psyche could be when in impossible situations. It was a strange feeling but was definitely preferable to the apprehension and fear that had crippled her for so long. At least now, with her more controlled manner, she could act rationally and make this whole state of affairs that little bit easier.

All of a sudden, a mighty crash thundered throughout the house causing Sara to jolt with surprise. *What on earth was that?* Sitting up on the edge of her bed, she listened as Michael emitted an ear piercing yell that reverberated throughout the house, followed by further crashing and banging. Sara sat stunned, listening to the commotion downstairs – he had lost it! Something had happened, something he didn't like... She had never known him to lose control out of the blue, she had usually been the cause. Was she concerned about him? The thought made her shudder and she quickly pushed it to the back of her mind.

Silence had fallen across the house, an eerie, contrasted silence to the abrupt outburst just moments ago. Was he ok? What had happened? She guessed she was about to find out as she could hear his soft footsteps downstairs, the volume increasing as he headed towards the staircase and began his ascent. She stood in the centre of the room staring at the door, apprehensively awaiting his appearance. He had never had an outburst of this magnitude in her presence and she had no idea what to expect when he came through the door. The lock clicked, the door opened, and Micahel entered with a smile on his face.

'Hello, Little Lamb!' he exclaimed.

Sara stood still, tense and unmoving. 'Are you OK? She asked tentatively.

'Oh I don't know, my Little Lamb. I am and I'm not. I don't really know how to feel. Apparently, we're not important anymore, not worthy of their time or their effort.' He was talking at a frantic, breathless pace which made her feel even more nervous.

'Has… has something ha-happened?' she stammered.

Michael's face was serious now, the previous smile wiped from his expression and he responded. 'A lot has happened, my dear girl. You see, they're not looking for us anymore, that's it. Done. They don't care where you are or who you're with and they certainly don't care who I am.' His voice seemed to have an air of disappointment but she wasn't certain, it didn't make any sense. Surely this was good news for him? She watched as he began to pace the room, irritated. He hadn't been completely clear but she was certain she knew where this was going, she just needed confirmation.

'Who doesn't care about us, Michael?'

'The police, of course! They've given up. They're no longer looking for us! The police don't care, your parents don't care, we will be forgotten about before you know it.' He paused and grinned at her. 'But at least we still have each other.'

Sara forced a smile, which felt more like a grimace, she was baffled, they were giving up? That was it? The police, her parents, they were just... *giving up?* She could feel the bile rising from her empty stomach and resisted the intense urge to vomit. Was she really worth so little that her own parents were giving up on finding her? What made it worse was he seemed *disappointed!* He had gotten away with taking her, ruining her life and he seemed disappointed? None of this made any sense.

Michael watched as Sara digested this news and could see the sadness on her face, he of all people knew what it was like to feel abandoned, to feel unwanted. He approached her, his arms outstretched and awkwardly offered up a hug. Sara looked at him cautiously, in all this time he had never tried any sort of affectionate physical contact and against her instincts, she accepted. She slipped into his arms and he wrapped her up tightly, his chin resting on the top of her head. It was the first positive human contact she had experienced in so long and she relaxed into his embrace. Allowing herself to feel her emotions, she began to sob into his shirt and, as he squeezed her even tighter, she had the realisation that, in his arms, she felt somewhat safe.

CHAPTER 27

Staring down at the chaos on his desk, Scott shook his head – it was an absolute shambles. The entire surface of his work surface was obscured by an array of unorganised paperwork and open files. To an unknowing eye, it served the illusion that he was immersed in his work but the reality was that he just didn't care anymore. The mess was an assortment of statements and evidence that he should've finalised and sorted by now but he was distracted, distracted by the one case he was no longer allowed to work.

It had been two weeks since the Sara Williams abduction case had been downgraded to low priority and he just couldn't let it go. It baffled him that they could just give up on a human life, a friend, a daughter; he couldn't just give up that easily. When instructed to pack away anything to do with the case, he had taken what he needed home and sent the remaining items to the file room. He wasn't going to give up looking for Sara, he couldn't!

With his focus being elsewhere, his current work had fallen to the wayside, he had been largely unhelpful to his colleagues, making excuses when they needed him and ignoring the more pressing paperwork that crossed his desk. The quality of his work was diminishing and he hadn't even gotten any closer to a breakthrough in finding Sara, it was an abhorrent situation to be in.

Forcing himself to put Sara to the back of his mind, he attempted to concentrate and make some sense of the disorder in front of him. A couple of high priority cases that required his urgent attention were being ignored, colleagues waiting on his help and he really couldn't care less. His usual drive to solve every case he was put on was long gone, for the first time in his career he was questioning the police system and the way they would classify certain cases, certain lives! How could you just quit when things got a little difficult? Budgets and resources becoming more important than a living person was an eventuality that he couldn't grasp.

Shoving the paperwork to one side, yet again, he stood up, vacated his desk and headed through to the break room to grab a coffee. The machine hummed into life once he had selected what he wanted and he waited patiently as his cup was filled. Once ready, he sipped tentatively at the hot drink, the boiling liquid burning his lips and tongue. Turning away from the machine, he made to leave the break room but found his exit obstructed by his superintendent, Nick Wilson.

'A quick word please, Scott.' Nick's tone was serious and he turned on a sixpence and marched towards his office without waiting for a reply.

Scott followed obediently, perplexed as to why he was suddenly being summoned into Nick's office. As he wandered between the desks of his colleagues, he was very aware that all eyes were on him; some stares were blatant, others more subtle and the whole situation made him feel a little uneasy.

When he reached his superior's office, Nick had already taken his place behind his desk, his expression pensive.

'Please close the door and have a seat, Scott.' Nick gestured lazily towards one of the unoccupied chairs on the opposite side to where he was sitting. Scott took one of the seats, the atmosphere in the room making him feel on edge – he had a feeling this was going to be a conversation he wasn't going to enjoy.

'I think it's about time we had a chat, Sergeant, but I want you to listen, not talk.' he paused and Scott nodded to show that he understood.

'It's no secret that the abduction case had a large, detrimental effect on you but it seems that it is now affecting all your other work. It's been brought to my attention on several occasions now by your colleagues, who feel as though your mind is elsewhere. You're not completing your tasks and you're not being helpful to any of your colleagues and I can't let this sort of behaviour continue when we have other cases that need solving.' Nick stopped again, took a deep breath and carried on. 'It's for these reasons that I have come to the decision to suspend you indefinitely, with pay, effective immediately. We will organise an assessment in a few weeks to see if you're fit to return but I need you to take this time to sort yourself out. Please turn in your badge, Sergeant.'

Scott sat still, shocked and dumbfounded, this was unexpected. He never envisioned that he would be relieved of his duties, even with the quality of his work plummeting rapidly. Standing up, almost in a trance, he removed his detective badge from his pocket, gently placed it on Nick's desk and exited the office. He walked back to his desk, ignoring the knowing stares and murmuring, gathered his personal belongings and left.

He was in a daze as he walked through the station and out into the fresh, cold air; the sun was shining and he squinted as his eyes adjusted to the natural light. Calmly, he wandered towards his vehicle and assessed his new situation. This time could actually be a blessing, he could channel all his energy into Sara's abduction. He was going to find her, prove everybody wrong and finally have the closure that he craved.

CHAPTER 28

November 2019

Yawning and stretching, Scott Harris awoke from a deep, alcohol induced slumber, his head was pounding and his mouth was as dry as a bone. He rolled over gently and slowly, movement making his headache throb more intensely, and reached over to his bedside table where last night's unfinished whisky stood. Grabbing the glass, he pounded it in one gulp, the alcohol scorching his throat and making his eyes water. Sitting up, he buried his head in his hands and cursed his hangover, with the amount he drank you would've thought he'd be immune by now!

He swung his legs out of bed and stood up unsteadily, stretching a second time, his body shuddering with the sensation. Stumbling clumsily across the bedroom, he ripped open the curtains, bathing the room in the unexpected, bright, autumnal sunshine. A delicate frost lay on the ground outside, making his driveway shimmer as if it was covered in thousands of diamonds. He stood for a moment, savouring the comforting warmth of the sunlight, enjoying the sensation on his skin.

Leaving the warm beam of light, he walked through to his bathroom and turned on the shower before taking his morning pee. Finishing up, he left the toilet unflushed as he didn't want to interfere with the shower and entered into the stream of hot water, hoping he would be able to wash away this hangover. As the hot water ran down his body, waking him up fully and invigorating him, he pondered what he could do to occupy himself for the day. Finding a new job would be productive but he dismissed the idea – that could wait for now.

It had been almost two years since he last worked for the police force. After spending several weeks suspended, they had arranged a meeting to re-evaluate his suspension and negotiate a possible return to work but Scott had failed to show. Too busy trying to continue his own personal investigation into Sara Williams' disappearance, he had completely forgotten about the meeting and they had sacked him without a second thought. Scott had spent the next year and a half burning through his savings in his continuing quest to find Sara, until finally calling it quits just six months prior. In that year and a half, he had chased dead end after dead end, not getting any closer to finding the missing girl. Giving up his search hadn't been an easy decision, quitting went against everything he believed in and depression had quickly set in. He spent weeks on end shut away in his house, in the dark, unwilling to engage in any attempt to rebuild his life. Alcohol was his answer and he guzzled scotch like it was going out of fashion.

Stepping out of the shower, he dried himself quickly with a rough towel before brushing his teeth. Looking at himself in the mirror, he despised the broken man that stared back at him. A failure, a drunk and a recluse – he wasn't even half the man he used to be. Once a formidable figure with a muscular, powerful physique, he was now frail and scrawny thanks to a combination of his liquid diet and no exercise; his dark hair had thinned and, along with his beard, carried flecks of grey – souvenirs from a stressful and exhausting few years. Age had crept on him quickly and his appearance was a constant reminder of his mistakes and his wasted existence.

Turning away from the stranger in the mirror, he walked back through to his bedroom, pulled on some boxers and his robe and headed downstairs. He promptly made himself a coffee and quickly tidied away the remnants from last night's microwave dinner. The bottle of whisky that he drank the night before lay empty and on its side on the kitchen worktop and he threw it away before grabbing a fresh bottle from the cupboard. Pulling the cork from the bottle with a satisfying pop, he added a generous measure to his coffee and enjoyed the scent permeating from the mug. Grabbing a cigarette from a crumpled pack and picking up his lighter, he headed towards the front of his house. He had recently started having his morning coffee and cigarette on his doorstep, there was something therapeutic about watching the world go by.

Opening the front door he was immediately greeted, once again, by the comfortable warmth of the late autumn sunshine; it was a beautiful day, the blue sky cloudless and vibrant and the air was crisp and refreshing, devoid of any breeze. Putting the cigarette to his lips, he lit it and drew in a lungful of smoke. The feeling of the nicotine hit was welcome, the uncomfortable, rasping cough as he exhaled was not. Trying to wash the feeling from his throat, he took a big gulp of his scotch-infused coffee. He followed that with a second, more reserved drag of his cigarette and blew the smoke out into the frosty air. He watched as the smoke dispersed slowly and disappeared and as the cloud finally dissipated fully, his attention was drawn to someone standing opposite his house on the street corner.

The gentleman, clutching a coffee of his own in a takeaway cup, was staring straight at him and Scott had the weirdest feeling that he had seen this stranger somewhere before. The man was of a slender build and tall, even from a distance, Scott could see his angular frame poking through his beige 'bomber' jacket. Scott stared back at him for a moment, his brain working overtime trying to figure out where he had crossed paths with this man before. He looked familiar, *very* familiar. Suddenly, the stranger noticed Scott was watching him and his entire manner changed, he stiffened up and looked in a state of panic. Scott's instincts kicked in, he had to talk to this man and he began to march across the street towards him; his approach was slowed by an oncoming vehicle in the road and the man took his opportunity and ran off, dropping his coffee cup as he scarpered.

Scott was baffled by the man's actions – that was some incredibly irregular behaviour! Unable to shake the feeling that he knew that man from somewhere, he collected the discarded coffee cup and headed back into his house. He might not be a detective anymore but you never lose that sixth sense and he knew the coffee cup could become important so he placed it in a sandwich bag and sealed it. Sitting down at his dining table, he racked his mind as to where he had seen this man before.

Out of nowhere, it came to him, it just clicked! He remembered where he and the stranger had met before! Rushing through to his office, he pulled out the box marked 'Sara Williams' and began frantically rooting through the contents. The man had approached him once before, the morning they were searching the park where Sara disappeared, and he had asked to help. Scott just needed confirmation that he was correct. He searched through statements, looked at the crime scene photos and photos from the search – nothing. He had the register of everyone who had helped on the search but there were many names on there and he had no way of singling out this individual. Why was this man here all of a sudden? Was he just some weird person who was obsessed with the case or was this more sinister? Could this be the breakthrough that he had been chasing all this time? Had it just fallen into his lap? He had to find out who this man was, he needed a name and he needed a conversation with him.

Going back through to the kitchen, he picked up the sealed sandwich bag that contained the stranger's coffee cup – it was time to call in a favour.

CHAPTER 29

Parking his vehicle along a residential road, Michael switched off the engine and removed his glasses to wipe the lenses before placing them back on his narrow nose and adjusted them so they were comfortable. He hadn't noticed the smears on them when he had left the house, it wasn't until the bright sunshine revealed them on the drive that they had been brought to his attention and bothered him for the rest of the journey.

It was an incredibly sunny, frosty morning; the air was icy and enlivening. He sipped at a cup of coffee he had purchased on the way, relishing the sensation as the beverage warmed his entire body from the inside out. Exiting his vehicle, coffee in hand, he began to casually stroll towards his destination; there was no need to rush, he could just enjoy this beautiful autumn weather. He had parked several hundred yards from where he wanted to be, a contingency – he didn't want his vehicle to be seen or associated with him. It was a good ten minute walk in this chilly air but with the sun beaming down on him through a cloudless sky, it was a delightful way to start his day.

Smiling and amiably greeting passers by, they could be forgiven for thinking he was an upstanding member of society. One of his strongest traits in his adulthood – blending in. In short, fleeting moments he had a knack of making people feel comfortable. A quick, friendly smile; a warm, polite greeting usually returned but he knew he would be forgotten moments later. However, anyone who spent a significant amount of time in the company of Michael Thompson would notice his peculiar personality traits – it was why he kept human contact to a minimum, it was difficult to hide who he really was.

As he approached his destination, he began to question his own decision to be here. It wasn't his first visit and he knew he was playing with fire. The risk was unnecessary but was also an urge that, for some reason, he was unable to stifle. He was voluntarily putting himself in a precarious situation all in the search of the attention that he craved so desperately.

It had been a little over two years since the police lost interest in him, allowing him to get away with a crime and leaving him victorious. The issue he was having was that he had enjoyed the notoriety. He was the unknown villain, the innominate wrongdoer, the nameless malefactor and it was a role that made him feel redoubtable and fearsome. The feeling of power it gave him had become addictive and he was beginning to yearn for it. It was an outcome he had not foreseen, he always thought having his 'Little Lamb' would be enough. Now he had experienced a taste of infamy and he was hungry for more, a need that he was trying to satiate.

Finally arriving at his journey's end at a 'T-junction', he stood on the street corner and stared across the road, coffee firmly grasped in his slender hand. His focal point, the home of former Detective Sergeant Scott Harris. Michael, like most of the country, had watched and read about the high profile dismissal of this once great detective and couldn't help but feel a little forlorn; this man was a formidable foe and without him in the hunt, life had become a little stale.

Michael had been here several times now, rarely seeing the ex-detective but revelling in the rush it gave him to be that close, almost taunting his old adversary. Glancing up at the house from his vantage point across the street, he was shocked to see Scott in one of the upstairs windows. Michael shifted a little, ready to leave, but the ex-detective's eyes were trained downward toward his rapidly thawing, ice-covered car and driveway. Michael relaxed and took a swig of his coffee, watching intently as Scott turned away from the window and disappeared out of sight.

Michael's pulse was racing – this was exhilarating! Merely a streets-width away from the man who was once tasked with trying to find him. Things had become a little dull for Michael recently and this was exactly what he needed – a little thrill. Taking another glug of his increasingly tepid coffee, he turned to leave, satisfied with this morning's exploits. Just as he turned to begin the walk back to his car, there was movement in the corner of his eye. Turning back to face Scott's house once more, he saw the man himself standing on his doorstep, lighting a cigarette.

Standing transfixed, Michael stared at his former nemesis and smiled to himself. This wasn't the tough-looking, intimidating man he had come face-to-face with years before. This man was run-down and beaten looking – Michael had ruined him, he had ended his career and now he stood less than fifty yards away, making a mockery of him. At that very moment, Michael felt content and accomplished. The sheer arrogance of standing right here in front of the detective who had been touted as one of the most successful in the country, the one who had lost everything trying to find him, was a bold move. He had been lost in his own little world for a few moments and turned his attention back to Scott, who was staring straight at him! He froze for a moment as the smugness was replaced by panic. Fuck! Scott had begun marching towards him. *Fuck!*

Michael decided he had overstayed his welcome and, as a perfectly-timed vehicle created a barrier between them, he turned and bolted, dropping his coffee in the process. Running as if his life depended on it, which in this instance it did, he didn't look back. The freezing air burned his throat and lungs as he breathed heavily, he hadn't run this much in years!

Reaching his vehicle, he quickly unlocked it and got in, slamming the door behind him. Looking back the way he came, he relaxed, no sign of Scott Harris. Allowing himself a few moments for his heart rate to calm down, he cursed himself. Had he just opened the door to being found out all in the name of a cheap thrill?

Turning the ignition of his 4x4, the engine chugged to life and he pulled away, still furious with himself. He had lived in constant conflict for the last few years, battling his need for anonymity with his craving for recognition. He thought he had these urges under control, thought he had found a way to cope with these impulses, but he had proved himself wrong today.

He smacked the steering wheel in temper, growing increasingly frustrated with his own actions. He would have to lay low for a while now, return to his normal life and blend in like he always had. Scott would have smelled blood today, Michael knew that, he was too smart to ignore this incident. The apprehension and fear was beginning to make him feel sick, he had executed everything up to this point so perfectly. He could've just left it alone, he should've been content with getting away with it.

He drove in silence, the radio turned off, his mind going a hundred miles an hour. He needed to use this time to calm down, there was no need to panic just yet. Deciding not to return to the house where Sara was, he headed back to his flat; if Scott had decided to follow him, there was nothing that could incriminate him there and Scott would have no right to question him.

Pulling up outside his flat and parking his usual spot, he turned off the engine and took a long, deep breath in through his mouth and exhaled out of his nose. Time to wake up a little and be more intelligent, more cautious. Today had been a close call, *too* close and he had to learn from it.

Pleased with his approach to the circumstances, he settled down and relaxed. He had to mitigate the situation he had created today, it was time to fade away again and hope that his desire for a little adventure didn't end up being his downfall.

CHAPTER 30

Pushing her untamed hair out of her face, irritated, Sara Williams closed the literature she was reading and placed the book on her bedside table; no use trying to read that without tying her mane out of the way. Sara hadn't had a haircut for over three years and, although it still suited her, the sheer volume of it had become a burden. She rummaged around her bedroom searching for a hair tie, the most elusive of items, eventually finding one under her bed. Tying her hair back out of her face, she grabbed her book and laid back down on her bed to continue reading. Bright sunshine was streaming through the bedroom window, the beam of warm light focussed perfectly on her spot on the bed and she lay in it like a sun-worshipping feline.

This was exactly how she had liked to start her day – slowly. She had awoken early, made a pot of coffee and returned to her room to read; for an hour she had laid there, ingesting every word in her book in the morning sunshine. These slow starts had become a routine she had grown to love. She hated to admit it but life was pretty easy right now; no responsibility, no bills, no mortgage. Being confined to this one building had its benefits.

Closing her book and putting it back on her bedside table, she reluctantly vacated the suntrap and put on her dressing gown. She grabbed her empty coffee mug, walked across the room, through the open bedroom door and headed downstairs – it was time to make breakfast. The hallway and staircase, although cleaner than when she first arrived, were still dusty and dank. She had battled to try and spruce it up but the mould was embedded in the floorboards and the dust seemed never ending. She wondered how long the house had been empty for before she got brought here but she didn't dare pry into Michael's personal life – she knew better than that. She walked down the stairs, a descent that was now silent thanks to Michael fixing the creaky stair treads and made her way to the kitchen.

The kitchen was one of three rooms she was now allowed unsupervised access to, her bedroom and the bathroom making up the trifecta. All other rooms remained locked at all times, for Michael to use only. She had taken pride in the three rooms she was allowed to use and, although not perfect, she had made them far more habitable. She busied herself making buttery toast, ensuring she cleaned up as she went, Michael didn't appreciate it when she left an unnecessary mess.

Pouring herself a fresh coffee she took a seat at the small, beaten up dining table and devoured her toast, she hadn't realised how ravenous she was.

She sat for a few moments, gazing longingly out of the kitchen window towards the vast woodland. The weather looked beautiful and inviting, a rare dry day during the British Autumn. She had been on several walks with Michael, not always the most relaxing as he always seemed a little on edge but she appreciated any time she could get outside. She sipped at her hot coffee and wondered if Michael would be back today, hoping he would be back today. If he did return, maybe he would let her join him for a walk; he probably would if she asked really nicely. She sat back and smiled to herself, content in the idea that in a few hours she could be wandering the woodland, in the fresh air – a small taste of freedom.

CHAPTER 31

As he reversed out of his driveway at speed, Scott felt sick with excitement and delight, he knew he was on to something. The man, the stranger turning up at the search and then being directly opposite his house was too much of a coincidence. Scott was certain he had his man, certain he had something to do with Sara's disappearance, he just had to call in a favour so he could find out more about him. The coffee cup, that had been dropped by the man and collected by Scott, sat on the passenger seat, still safely secured inside a ziplock sandwich bag. Scott was going to take it to his old boss and get them to run it for DNA. If the stranger was in the database, they would have their man. The anticipation was building inside of him, he was certain his perseverance was about to pay off. He had trusted his instincts and if he was right it was possible they could solve this case and hopefully give some closure to The Williams. It might even get him his job back.

He drove erratically towards the police station, weaving in and out of traffic and overtaking at every opportunity, time was of the essence. The quicker he got the cup to them, the sooner they would know who the man was. This was the closest thing they had had to a proper person of interest since Sara Williams went missing and it was something he was sure his old colleagues would not pass up.

Pulling up into an empty parking space in the 'visitors' section of the car park, he switched off the engine and then rested his head on the steering wheel, taking a long, deep breath. He stared across the car park at the building where he enjoyed so much success, he hadn't been in there since his dismissal. He hadn't seen or spoken to any of his former colleagues and here he was, turning up with information on the case that caused him to lose his job in the first place.

Stepping out of his vehicle, he fumbled around in his pockets for his cigarettes, a quick smoke would help him calm his nerves. Unable to find them in his pockets, he searched inside his car and cursed himself when he realised he must have left at home. Grabbing the coffee cup from the passenger seat, he slammed the car door in frustration. He took another deep breath, forced himself to calm down and began his march to his old place of work, coffee cup clutched in his hand.

As he tentatively entered the station, he was greeted with multiple looks of shock and disdain; former colleagues, eyes wide, unable to believe that the shamed detective would actually have the audacity to come through those doors. He could feel some of them looking him up and down, judging his appearance but he didn't pay any attention to them. Others, including the officer behind the front desk, froze in fear, waiting to see if he was here to cause a disturbance. Ignoring the stares and whispers, he approached the front desk and addressed the officer behind it.

'I need to see Superintendent Wilson' he exclaimed.

The officer behind the desk was someone Scott had worked with many times over the years and knew his reputation, he began to object.

'Look, Scott, I really don't thi-'

'Just get Nick. I'm not here to cause trouble but, I can tell you, I won't be leaving until I have spoken to him.' The tone of Scott's voice was calm and controlled but carried a veiled threat that the officer recognised. Spinning around in his chair, he picked up the phone and called through to the superintendent. Scott stood and waited patiently as the people around him stopped watching and continued with their day, the drama seemingly over already. The officer behind the desk, whose name Scott couldn't recall, was still watching him warily and he forced a smile across his face to try and ease the tension. The awkward silence was broken by the familiar sound of the security doors that led to his former workplace opening, followed by the sound of Nick's footsteps as he made his way down the corridor. Scott peered round the corner to see his former superior walking towards him, his face an expression of contempt.

'Scott. What can we do for you?' Nick's voice was flat and uninterested.

Scott deliberately ignored the tone and went straight to the point.

'Nick, I think I've had a breakthrough in the Sara Williams case, it literally fell into my lap! This morning, I had a man watching me from across the street and I knew I'd seen him somewhere before! Then it just clicked! He approached me at the initial search, after we had sent everyone away, don't you think that's suspicious?' The question was rhetorical and Scott continued talking at a breathless pace. 'When he saw me looking back at him he panicked and ran off, again very strange behaviour! He dropped this coffee cup which we should run for DNA. I just think this is all too much to just be a coincidence, I think we have our man!' Scott finally stopped and took a breath, holding the bag containing the cup out towards his former boss.

The silence that followed Scott's word vomit was awkward and people had stopped, once again, to listen to what was going on. Nick stood shocked and wide eyed, ignoring the outstretched coffee cup. Scott allowed Nick a moment to digest this new information, this sudden breakthrough. He stood, smiling, waiting for the positive response that was inevitably coming. However, Nick rolled his eyes and pushed the coffee cup back towards Scott.

'For Christ's sake, Scott, this again?' it was said in a frustrated whisper but the volume of his voice began to rise as he continued. 'You have ruined your career, alienated the few friends you had, made a mockery of this department and you're still unable to let this go? You're an embarrassment, mate.' Leaning toward Scott, he lowered his voice so even Scott could barely hear. 'It's been three years, Scott, the girl is dead. Leave it alone.' His voice returned to a normal register. 'Now, please take your litter and leave my station, we have real cases to work on.' With that, Nick turned on his heel and walked away.

Scott stood, perplexed, he couldn't comprehend what had just happened. Nick had just completely dismissed him, he hadn't even entertained for a moment that Scott could be right. He stood for a moment, dejected and disappointed, before taking his coffee cup and leaving the station. Once outside, he shivered against the cold, his shoulders slumped and his mood deflated. He had tried but that was it, he couldn't keep going through this sort of disappointment. Trudging back to his car, he felt defeated, the earlier elation of thinking he had a breakthrough felt like a distant memory.

As he made his journey back to his vehicle, he passed a rubbish bin and made to throw the coffee cup away but felt a hand grab his wrist and stop him. He spun around to see who the hand belonged to.

'Lock?' He was surprised to see his former subordinate, who was now a Sergeant.

'Hi Scott' he smiled. 'Look, I don't have long and no one can see me doing this but I heard what just went on, give me the cup.'

'Why?' Scott asked, confused.

Lock snatched the cup from Scott's hand. 'I'll get it looked at, just wait for my call. I'll try and get it rushed through but it'll still be a few days, as you know. Right, I have to go.' With that, he turned, concealing the coffee cup under his jacket and rushed back towards the station.

Scott smiled and felt optimistic once more. Who would've thought young Lock would be the one to help him? It was a surprising turn of events but it had resulted in what he wanted. Now he just had to wait for the results and hope it was information he could use. Getting back into his vehicle, he sat and allowed the events to sink in – had he finally done it? Turning the key in the ignition, he pulled out of his space and began his journey home. He had a few days until he got the results but he was certain this was it and he needed to prepare. It was time to sort himself out, get organised and do what he was good at.

CHAPTER 32

Sara was bored. It had been five long days since she had last seen Michael and the tedium of solitude had rendered her irate. How *dare* he leave her locked inside alone for this long! She idly rearranged the books on her bookshelf, it was an unnecessary task but it kept her occupied, and then slumped down onto her bed, frustrated. Michael hadn't once mentioned that he was planning on being away from the house for this long, it was an unfair surprise. The weather had been unseasonably warm and sunny for the last few days and she had been shut inside the entire duration, she was beginning to go stir crazy! She had tried keeping herself busy; firstly by reading and losing herself in the world of fiction; secondly by attempting to attack the filthy hallway again, desperate to get rid of the damp. It hadn't worked and the aroma of the cleaning products hung thick in the air, stinging her nostrils.

Getting up, she made her way downstairs, it was almost lunchtime and her stomach was rumbling. Opening the kitchen cupboards, she cursed Michael again, she was almost out of food! 'He better have a bloody good excuse when he gets back!' she thought to herself, searching the barren cupboards for any form of sustenance. Fortunately, she located the last two slices of bread and went about making a jam sandwich, the feeling of annoyance still surging through her body.

As she sat down to eat her simple lunch, she heard the familiar low rumble of a vehicle coming down the track. Abandoning the consumption of her sandwich, she rushed to the kitchen window in time to see Michael's 4x4 pull up into its usual spot on the perimeter of the woodland.

She watched as Michael exited his vehicle and made his way towards the house. His appearance shocked her; his clothes were wrinkled and messy, his usually neatly combed hair was sticking up in various directions and he looked tired and dishevelled, his eyes encircled by dark rings. He glanced at Sara peering at him through the window as he approached the entrance to the house but his customary affectionate smile was missing, replaced by a haunted look and he avoided making eye contact with her. Sara raced to the front door to meet him as he entered and didn't hesitate to question him as he stepped over the threshold.

'Where, the bloody hell, have you been?' she barked, not making any effort to hide her indignation.

Michael ignored the question and barged past her, none-too-gently, heading toward the sitting room. She watched as he fumbled around with his keys, trying to locate the one that would grant him access to the eternally locked room, his hands shaking violently making the task more troublesome than it should have been. Finally locating the key he needed, he unlocked the door and walked in, still having not uttered a single word.

Sara watched as he paced around the room, navigating through the stacks of newspapers he had hoarded over the years. His face was contorted into a mixed expression of dread and confusion and she began to worry. His behaviour was peculiar, even more so than usual, something must have happened. She opened her mouth to continue her inquisition but just as the words were on the edge of her lips, he shot her a look that warned her to hold her tongue. Silently, she obeyed and stood awkwardly in the doorway as he continued his frantic patrol of the sitting room.

Eventually ceasing his stomping around, he sat down in one of the dusty armchairs, placed his head in his hands and began mumbling incoherently. Sara leaned forward a little and strained her ears to listen but could only make out the occasional word. 'Stupid... why... ruined.' What on earth was he talking about? Kneeling down beside him, she gently placed a hand on his thigh but remained quiet. She just kept her hand on his leg, watching his body heaving with each deep, shuddering breath. She waited patiently, hoping he would calm down enough to tell her what had happened. Several minutes passed, Michael's panicked breathing getting gradually slower and more controlled. Sara hadn't moved from his side, hoping that her presence would help him to settle.

Finally, he lifted his head and looked her in the eyes. Sara smiled amiably, hoping his little episode had concluded. Whatever had happened in the last few days had taken its toll on her captor; he looked as though he had aged ten years, his eyes were gaunt and sunken into his skull, his lips were cracked and dry, and his entire demeanour was one of pure exhaustion. Staring at his face, she felt a pang of pity, a feeling she tried to suppress. Oftentimes she had fleeting moments of affection towards him, especially when he showed moments of vulnerability, but she battled those emotions furiously, reminding herself that he was not a good person. He was a fiend and a predator.

'I've... done something... stupid' he said suddenly, his voice sounded hoarse and raspy. 'Something that could ruin everything.'

Sara took his hand in hers. 'Whatever it is, we can fix it' she said, tenderly.

Michael was looking at her as she said it and he suddenly pulled her into his arms and kissed her on the mouth, forcefully. She didn't object to the kiss, that hadn't worked out well in the past. He had kissed her before, although these moments were few and far between. The last time she had resisted he had locked her in her room for days, his feelings clearly hurt. This time, however, she relaxed into it, somewhat grateful for the human contact. Pulling away from the embrace, Michael gazed at her lovingly.

'I may have ruined everything, Little Lamb. I went to the old detective's house, the one who was looking for you... I was just curious, I couldn't help it. He saw me... he definitely saw me and now they'll be looking for you again. They'll take me away from you!' Michael had blurted all this out at a frenzied pace.

Sara allowed herself a few moments to digest this sudden onslaught of information, confused and conflicted by the sudden turn of events. She had long given up any hope of going back to her old life. She decided the best course of action right now was to console him.

'Look, Michael, you're panicking. There's absolutely no need to panic yet. So what if he saw you? He still doesn't know who you are, he doesn't know your name. You're safe. Just *please* stop putting yourself in these silly situations.'

Michael had listened intently, hanging off her every word and she saw him visibly relax, the worry disappearing from his face to be replaced with a relieved smile. It seemed she had managed to allay his fears.

Once again, he pulled her in close, into a tight hug. She settled into his arms, her mind racing. There was finally a chance she could be found soon. The confusing part – she wasn't entirely sure she wanted to be.

CHAPTER 33

Sitting in his car, Scott stared out into the park he hadn't visited in almost two years – the park where Sara Williams had been taken. It was blowing a gale outside and his vehicle rocked gently as it was repeatedly buffeted by the howling wind. It was mid-afternoon and the park was practically empty; a lone dog walker strolled around the perimeter, staggering occasionally when battered by one of the powerful gusts, their treasured canine companion excitedly attacking leaves as they drifted down from the towering trees.

Scott waited for the dog walker to leave the park before stepping out of his car into the tempestuous wind, pulling on a jacket to protect himself from the elements. He stood for a moment, rooted to the spot, as if some invisible force was restraining him, stopping him from going into the park itself. The reality was that he was battling his own reluctance to return to the scene of his greatest failure. Taking a deep breath, he gathered the courage to take the first step and made his way towards the park entrance.

He wandered slowly on the park pathway, the same route he had taken the first time he had been here, retracing the last steps Sara had taken before going missing. A light, misty rain had started to fall and he zipped his jacket to the top to protect himself from becoming saturated. The park was quiet, he was alone and he ambled along the path at a conservative pace, taking it all in. He had returned here today to refamiliarise himself with the scene of the crime, it was a trigger to get himself into the necessary head-space. If he was about to finally crack this case, he wanted to know the scene inside out.

As he walked along the part of the pathway that ran adjacent to the woodland, he tried to envision how she had been taken, thinking it might help some-how. Had the kidnapper leapt out as she ran past? Did she stop to rest here, inadvertently making herself an easier capture? Questions he didn't know the answer to, he could merely speculate, but that didn't matter anymore. What mattered was that he found Sara and was finally able to give her family some closure. Finally give himself some closure.

Stopping at the area where they had determined she had been taken, you wouldn't have realised any-thing untoward had happened here. The foliage had regenerated in abundance and the whole area was now obscured, you would never know someone had experienced the most terrifying moment of their life in that exact spot.

Scott stood for a few moments, staring into the vegetation as if willing Sara to emerge and life to go back to normal. A futile thought, regardless of outcome, life would never feel the same as it once did. The rainfall had increased and Scott decided it was time to head back to his car, there was no need to just stand here and get drenched. As he walked back at a brisk pace, he was glad he had come back here. This park was a reminder of the biggest mistake of his decorated career, a mistake he was certain he was close to rectifying. That was if he found Sara alive… the alternative didn't even bear thinking about.

He broke into a trot for the final stretch to his vehicle, the rain getting heavier, and gratefully got in, sheltering from the downpour. Removing his saturated coat, he threw it on to the back seat and then turned on the ignition so the heating would kick in. He relaxed as he was enveloped in the warm air and closed his eyes for a moment. Suddenly his brief moment of tranquillity was punctuated by the shrill sound of his mobile phone ringtone. Grabbing his phone, he answered hastily when he saw 'James Lock' on the screen.

'Lock?'

'Alright mate.' It was a form of address, not a question. 'The DNA test came up with a match... a Michael Thompson.'

Excitement surged through Scott's body, he had a name! He had a lead! Stifling his elation, he listened as Lock continued.

'Colourful childhood, grew up in the foster system after his mother took her own life. Doesn't look as though the father was ever in the picture. Repeated hospital visits for 'accidents' but they were most likely beatings from the looks of the reports. I assume you want his last known address?'

'Yes! Please, yes!' Scott said eagerly and swiftly grabbed a pen and an old receipt to scribble it down on as Lock recited it to him. Scott was beyond grateful, it was more than he had bargained for but before he could articulate that to Lock, his former colleague was speaking again.

'That's it from me, Scott. Remember, whatever comes from this try and leave my name out of it.' With that, the line went dead.

Scott stared down at the crumpled receipt on which he had scrawled the address, this was it! Inputting the location into his sat-nav, he backed out of his parking space and began his journey to Michal Thompson's home.

. . .

Pulling up on the side of the road, opposite the address he had been given, Scott looked across the street towards the potential home of his first proper person of interest. The sun was setting and twilight had descended, turning the sky a deep blue before it descended into inevitable darkness, but he could still just about make out the flat number he was looking for. His vantage point was a good one, well chosen. Parked along the street with a plethora of other vehicles, he wouldn't stand out and he also had an unobstructed view of Michael Thompson's front door. There were no lights on and the parking space outside was vacant, one could only assume he wasn't home.

Scott adjusted his seat to give himself space to stretch out and made himself comfortable. Just because the man he was looking for wasn't here didn't mean he was going to leave, he would wait it out. It had been three, long years waiting for this moment, what difference would a few more hours make?

CHAPTER 34

Locking the heavy, wooden front door behind him, Michael walked outside into the damp air. A gentle breeze blew causing the pine trees to groan and their needles fissile in the wind, other than that he was greeted by a complete and eerie silence. As he approached his vehicle he was calm, it had been several days since his altercation with the former detective and he had spent most of that time stressed and full of worry. Sara had managed to somewhat placate his previous dread, suggesting he just stay there with her for a few days until they could be certain he hadn't attracted any unwanted attention. He had been fretting about his situation and a few days with his 'Little Lamb' seemed like the ideal solution. Although reluctant to leave her at all, he had to head back to grab clothes and necessities and would call in sick to work the day after.

Climbing into his vehicle, he pulled away and began the short journey along the rutted dirt track to the main road. Droplets of rain were beginning to plunge from the gloomy skies and he flicked on the windscreen wipers to combat the moisture's attempt at obscuring his vision. Reaching the end of the track he paused for a moment, ensuring the roads were empty and only then did he turn on his headlights. The roads were always quiet around here, it was so remote but he always made sure he was cautious to not draw any attention as he came away from his hidden residence.

Beginning his journey, he savoured the peacefulness. The strain he had put on himself over the last few days had rendered him exhausted and he was looking forward to returning to his love and laying low for a few days. Maybe this scare was the wake up call he needed, maybe it was time he took Sara somewhere new, somewhere they could begin their life together. He smiled to himself as he pondered the thought. He *deserved* a normal life, some peace and happiness. His entire life had been a turbulent mess of disorder, tragedy and sadness and he was finally close to achieving a feeling of contentment. Perhaps a new location, a new life with Sara would complete that. A chance to put their unconventional beginnings behind them and start afresh.

The hour-long journey back to his flat flew by, his mind consumed by thoughts of a clean slate. He hadn't even noticed the increase in traffic as he approached the populous area of urban life. The rain was now hammering down relentlessly, the din deafening as the precipitation slammed against the exterior of his 4x4. Dusk was falling and the calming cloak of darkness was approaching. Soon the tumbling array of grey clouds would be replaced by the natural camouflage of night, allowing him to move around with more obscurity.

Finally pulling up outside his flat, he pulled into his parking space and switched off the headlights and then the engine. The street lights were casting long shadows across the rain-soaked ground, the amber light shimmering in the ever expanding puddles. Yanking his coat up over his head to protect himself from the torrential downpour, he exited his vehicle and hastily rushed to his front door. He unlocked it quickly and practically leapt through the entrance into the dry sanctuary of his home. Removing his saturated coat, he hung it up, entered his kitchen and set up filling a reusable shopping bag with supplies.

Once he had gotten what he needed from the kitchen, he made his way through to his immaculate bedroom and began to fill a small suitcase with clothes – just enough to last him for a few days. He then placed everything by the front door, ready to be loaded into the car.

Returning to his small kitchen, he flicked on the kettle and prepared himself a cup of tea before taking a seat at his two-seat dining table in the corner of the room. Tentatively sipping at the hot liquid, he felt gratified with his new plan. He needed to fight the urge for attention from strangers, it was a headspace he shouldn't allow himself to get into. All he needed was his 'Little Lamb' and for them to begin an actual life together, something he would discuss with her when he got back. He was certain she would go for it, her whole persona had changed during their time together – he always knew she would see sense eventually. The start of their relationship wasn't exactly romantic but it was the only way and it had worked out, they now enjoyed each other's company a vast amount. He would have to find somewhere new for them both, somewhere away from here and take her there first. He could sell his two properties afterwards which would give them more than enough money to live on. He smiled again at his plan, already looking forward to his new life.

Finishing his tea, he uncharacteristically left the unwashed mug in the sink and made his way into the hallway. He threw on his coat, grabbed his belongings and stepped out into the rain, this time relishing the refreshing feeling, closing and locking the front door behind him. Strolling around to the rear of his vehicle, he loaded his belongings into the back and ensured they were secure, humming a happy, upbeat tune the whole time. This was possibly the first time in his life he felt truly carefree, almost completely untroubled. Closing the back door, he made his way to the driver's side and got in, humming away and completely unaware that at that very moment he was being watched.

CHAPTER 35

Clutching a steak slice in one hand and a takeaway coffee in the other, Scott cursed as he exited the petrol station – the skies had opened and it was pouring with rain... and he had walked there. Having been sitting in his vehicle for several hours watching the address Lock had given him, the engine switched off to avoid attracting attention, he had developed a craving for some hot food and drink. Not wanting to give up his ideally situated vantage point, he had left his vehicle where it was and made the short journey to the services, on foot, to quench his hankering. When he departed his car the weather had been dry, now the rain was lashing down and he was going to get soaked! A development that irked him massively.

He set off on his short walk back to his BMW at a brisk pace, wanting to get out of the rain as soon as possible. The stroll was not enjoyable, the rain slammed harshly against his face, aided by the wind, and his shoes quickly revealed themselves to be pervious. By the time he got back to his vehicle he was drenched and incredibly uncomfortable, not an ideal eventuality when he was going to be sat in his car for an uncertain amount of time. 'That's what I get for leaving my coat behind' he said out loud as he pressed the key fob to open his car.

Settling back into the driver's seat, his eyes trained back on the front door of Michael Thompson's supposed residence, he devoured his rapidly cooling savoury treat, chewing ferociously – he was famished! The parking space outside was still vacant and he hoped his suspect hadn't been and gone in the short duration he was absent. Taking a large glug of his coffee, which was now optimum drinking temperature, he mentally prepared himself for what could be a very long night. He had no idea how long he was going to be here and if he was completely honest with himself, he didn't care – he would wait as long as it took.

Reclining his seat a little, he made himself more comfortable and then switched the radio on. The soothing tones of *James Bay* filled his ears and he smiled. 'The calm before the storm' he thought to himself. He had no idea what was going to happen if and when he saw his suspect, he would have to rely on instinct as he so often had. As the *James Bay* song faded out to be replaced by *Little Mix,* Scott could feel his eyelids getting heavier. Battling the urge to take a nap, he gulped down another mouthful of coffee and forced himself to open his eyes wide. Sleep would have to wait, he couldn't afford to risk missing out on this opportunity.

As he forced himself to be more alert, a vehicle caught his eye; an old Land Rover Discovery had just pulled into the car park he was watching over. It was the first vehicle he had seen come or go since he got there and he watched with an unwavering stare as the 4x4 slowly navigated the car park and pulled into the empty space he had been observing. Scott sat bolt upright, returning his seat to its original position. His gaze was fixed on this anonymous vehicle like a feline stalking an oblivious bird. A mixture of excitement, apprehension and anticipation surged through his body and he gaped fervently as a figure exited the vehicle – this is the moment he had been waiting for.

Unfortunately for Scott, the person stepped out into the rain with their jacket awkwardly pulled up over their head, inadvertently hiding their face. Scott stared unblinking, hoping to catch a glimpse of their face to confirm their identity but, to his dismay, they rushed straight into the flat. This may have been Michael Thompson's address but he needed visual confirmation. All he could decipher so far was that they were definitely male.

Scott smacked the steering wheel in frustration, if that was his suspect turning in for the night he would have to wait here all night and get confirmation in the morning. Scott was absolutely livid, what were the chances of him unknowingly obscuring his face? The former detective's vexation grew further the longer he sat there and he toyed with the idea of knocking on the door of the flat. An internal suggestion that he cast aside quickly, revealing himself and having no authority to apprehend the man would be disastrous. He had to remain patient and wait it out.

Thirty-five minutes passed by, each one feeling longer than the previous, and there was no further movement. Scott would have to stay up all night to ensure he didn't miss his window – he sighed at the thought, already exhausted. He decided he may as well make himself comfortable again, he was going to be here for the long haul, but just as he settled, movement outside the flat captured his attention once more. The front door swung open and the man stepped outside carrying a bag and a suitcase, his jacket worn as normal with his head uncovered. Scott strained his eyes as he stared intently at the man and as he stepped into the streetlight his face was revealed. Glasses, harsh, angular features and a long, pointed nose; the same face that had spoken to Scott at the park, the same face that had been outside his house, the face that belonged to Michel Thompson.

Scott watched as Michael loaded the two bags into the back of his old 4x4 and then climbed back behind the wheel. *He was leaving already?* He backed out of his parking space and drove from the car park. *Where the fuck was he going?* Scott knew he had to follow, he couldn't just let him drive off into the night. Turning on the engine of his BMW, he waited until Michael had driven down the main road a short distance before pursuing, allowing enough space between the two vehicles to ensure he didn't alert his suspect.

As he followed, he became increasingly anxious. This was a development he hadn't anticipated and he had no real plan of how to approach Michael when he got the opportunity. The fact that he was on his own without any backup was becoming very apparent. All he knew was that he wanted this to end tonight, he had to detain him and question him, he *needed* closure. His heart was hammering away inside his rib cage, the sudden increase in heart rate was making him feel woozy and he took some deep, controlled breaths to try and calm himself and focus on the matter at hand.

They had been driving for a little over three quarters of an hour when Michael left the main road and turned down a remote country lane. Scott continued to follow, still maintaining a conservative distance between their two vehicles and he switched off his headlights. It was pitch black out here with very few buildings, if Michael was to see him he could become suspicious. However, the combination of the rain that was thumping down and no light to illuminate the road ahead, driving became progressively more challenging. He gripped the steering wheel tightly, his knuckles turning white, leaned forward and fixed his gaze upon the rear of Michael's 4x4. The rear lights were glowing red like the eyes of a demon leading him into the blackness and they gave him a focal point to help maintain his pursuit. The gap between their two vehicles had increased due to the necessary cautiousness of his approach and he reluctantly increased his speed, worried he may fall too far behind his suspect. The level of concentration he was having to use on this journey was making his head pound but he ignored the discomfort, it would be worth it in the end. He was so close to a resolution he could taste it.

Turning a sharp bend on the narrow country lane, he came to a long straight where he could see the illuminated rear of Michael's vehicle once more. Pressing on the accelerator a little, he closed the gap, still careful not to get too close. Suddenly the brake lights lit up on the 4x4 and it took a sharp left turn into the dense woodland that surrounded them. Startled by the unexpected deviation off of the road Scott put his foot down, his breathing becoming erratic as the panic rose inside him – had he been seen?

As he neared the rough area where Michael had turned, he slowed right down to scan the area. On his left a dirt track appeared, almost unnoticeable if you were driving at a normal speed. A large sign that said 'PRIVATE' was nailed to one of the massive Scots pine trees that loomed overhead. Some way down the track he could see the rear lights of Michael's vehicle moving violently in the darkness. Scott drove straight past the turning and pulled over in a safe spot a short distance beyond the track entrance, there was absolutely no way he could drive down there without his lights on and turning them on would inevitably lead to his detection. Pulling his phone out of his pocket, he opened up the 'maps' application to have a look at where the track went and the image he was greeted with made his breath catch in his throat. Using his thumb and index finger in a pincer movement, he zoomed in on the image to make sure he was seeing it correctly. At the end of the track, which was roughly a couple hundred yards in length, was a clearing; within that clearing, what looked like a house. A bloody house! In the middle of the woods? The stereotype would be amusing if the situation wasn't so serious.

He stared at his phone screen for several minutes, not quite able to believe his eyes – this had to be it! Was this where he had kept Sara? Was she still there? There was only one way to find out. Reaching over to the back seat, he grabbed his jacket and clumsily put it on inside the vehicle. The rain was still lashing down outside and he knew his only approach would be to walk through the dense woodland, aided by the blanket of darkness.

Climbing out of his vehicle, he closed the door behind him and stood for a moment as the droplets peppered him like miniature bullets from above. Staring out into the woodland, the cold and impregnable darkness that greeted him was unnerving and uninviting but there was no turning back now. He slowly walked around his vehicle and began his journey into the gloomy wilderness.

CHAPTER 36

Scott stood at the entrance to the house, staring into the dimly lit hallway that was partially irradiated by the light from the kitchen. He was absolutely soaked from the trek through the woodland, the rain only ceasing moments before. His clothes were sodden, heavy with rain water and the weight was forcing his posture into a less than comfortable position. His dark hair, once full and luscious, had been flattened to his head by the downpour, giving him the appearance of a wet dog, blood from blackthorn cuts mixed with the rainwater on his face, making him look even more bloodied than he actually was. The precarious route he had taken amongst the trees had rendered him completely saturated, filthy and chilled to the bone but the adrenaline that was now surging throughout his body was masking the discomfort. Standing still, almost statuesque, he stared through the open doorway into the building, still astonished that the door had been unlocked. However, he was under no illusion that this entire night would be that easy and he was as prepared as he could be for what was to come. Still rooted to the spot, he realised just how frightened he was and the fear had him frozen. The enormity of the circumstance he had himself in became increasingly apparent. Maybe he should have called for help but the chances of anyone actually taking him seriously were slim and he couldn't waste this opportunity.

Taking a deep breath, his lungs filling with the crisp, wintry air, he counted to ten in his head, forcing himself to calm down. He exhaled, his shoulders drooping back into their original position, summoned every ounce of courage he had and took his first step into the house.

As he planted his foot on the old, wooden floor, the boards let out a harsh, unhelpful groan under his weight. Pausing and gritting his teeth, he held his breath and listened intently, worried he had alerted his target with his first movement. A few moments passed, his heart thumping so vigorously he could feel it in his ears. Wind swirled around hauntingly outside, drops of water running from the roof of the house and smattering on the damp ground. These were the only sounds, however, and once satisfied he hadn't unintentionally announced his arrival, he took another cautious step into the house and very gently closed the door behind him.

Creeping a little further into the house, his water-logged shoes squelched with each nervous, hesitant step. He was greeted by the strong scent of damp, that made him scrunch his nose in disgust. The scent was mingled in with something else, something chemical, a cleaning product perhaps. Sniffing at the air a few times, he came to the horrifying realisation that it was bleach. Bleach! His stomach churned and sank, in his career he only ever associated bleach with one thing and it wasn't positive. Had there been a clean up after a crime here? After a… death? Gulping anxiously, he shut his eyes and forced the thought out of his mind, it didn't bear thinking about – he had to believe Sara was still alive.

Opening his eyes, he forced himself to focus on the matter at hand. The light that was pouring from the kitchen partially illuminated his surroundings and he scanned the area, taking it all in. To his left, a closed door next to the staircase, directly opposite the kitchen door that was to his right. Adjacent to the stairs ran a hallway where he could see two more doors, both on the right; one closed, one open. Glancing up the stairs he could see some light creeping out from under a doorway and out into the landing, probably where his suspect was. Keeping his wits about him, he decided to take the opportunity to explore the downstairs, hoping Michael would stay out of the way for a little while.

Stepping forward, his first port of call was the closed door next to the stairs. Delicately, he placed his hand on the doorknob and turned it but was met with resistance – locked, how disappointing. Turning away from the secured room, he passed the kitchen and walked down the hallway, each step controlled and almost soundless. He tried the first door he came to past the kitchen, more luck with this one as the door opened with ease. Just a toilet, old, run-down and unmaintained – nothing of note in there. Rolling his eyes, he gingerly closed the door and continued his journey down the hallway. Reaching the final doorway that was already open, it made him raise the question as to why only one of these doors was secured. What was behind it that required it to be locked?

Approaching the end of the hallway, and the final door, he peered inside – a utility room. Glancing around as he walked in, it looked pretty standard, nothing untoward. He knelt down in front of the old washing machine and investigated the inside; it was empty but there were droplets of moisture clinging to the interior and he could smell fabric freshener. This has been used recently, he thought to himself standing back up and he looked around, hoping to to find some female clothing. Something, anything that could give him hope that Sara was still alive. No luck.

Across the room was another doorway that led to a small hallway and he went through to investigate. It just looked like a cramped entryway, no longer used;

the old door was secured with plywood and nailed shut. Opposite the door was a closet, a small wooden stool in front of it. Moving the stool, he opened the door and poked his head inside, nothing but cobwebs. Closing the door, he sat on the stool and collected his thoughts. He had been fruitless so far but there was something behind that locked door that his suspect didn't want to be easily accessed. The thought of what could lie beyond perturbed him and he stifled his imagination before it ran away with him.

Deciding there was nothing of worth downstairs that he could access, he knew his next step was to head upstairs towards his suspect. It was time. He crept along the hallway once more, ensuring Michael hadn't decided to come downstairs and stopped at the base of the staircase. He allowed himself a moment to get himself together before taking his first careful step towards the upper level.

He climbed the stairs, his terror mounting with every step and he fought the panic that was coursing through him. Never before had he been this afraid, this uncertain but there was no turning back, this was it. His ascension was slow and wary, his senses heightened within the silence. He remained vigilant as he approached the summit, fully aware that if Michael came out of the room now he would have the upper hand. The element of surprise was all he had right now and he wanted to utilise it fully, getting the jump on him could be the difference.

As he neared the top, edging towards the minute amount of light that was slithering out from underneath the doorway, he heard something. Halting a couple of steps from the landing, mere feet from his destination he listened intently – voices. Not one voice but two, a muffled conversation coming from the otherside of the door. Unable to make out any words, he took the last couple of steps and stood outside the doorway. Did he have someone helping him? An accomplice? No, that didn't fit, it didn't add up. He pressed his ear against the door, careful not to make a sound. A man was talking, chattering away as Scott listened and then the second voice responded, a female! Sara? Scott's stomach turned over, was that her? Was he a paltry few inches from the girl he had wanted to find all these years? The thought was incomprehensible.

He wrapped his hand around the door knob slowly and delicately, his palms sweating profusely. Ensuring he had a good grip and praying that the door wasn't locked from the inside, he twisted the knob and pushed. The door swung open, bathing him in artificial light. The sudden influx of brightness stung his eyes but once they adjusted he couldn't believe what he was seeing.

CHAPTER 37

Taking a left on to the ragged, uneven track, Michael was almost home. His car lurched from side to side as always, tossing him about roughly inside. It was a short, rough and tumble drive that he had grown to enjoy, it meant he was almost back with his love.

As he steadily traversed the potholed route, something in his rear-view mirror caught his attention. He could've sworn he'd seen movement! Slamming his brakes on, the 4x4 skidding slightly on the rain soaked ground, he brought the vehicle to a halt. He turned over his shoulder to get a getter look, gazing through the water spattered rear window to see if there was anything there. He was greeted by nothing but darkness and an empty track but he watched avidly for a few moments, just in case. Nothing.

Returning to face the front, he gripped the steering wheel tight and shook his head forcefully, as if physically trying to rattle the thought from his mind. Paranoia had been a problem over the last few days, understandably, and it was about time he calmed down. Out here in the middle of nowhere, he was safe, there was nothing to worry about.

Continuing on the final stretch of the track, he couldn't shake the feeling that he had seen something and it made him uneasy. Taking several deep breaths, he forced himself to relax, it was ridiculous. Even if something *had* moved behind him he was in the middle of a vast woodland, it was probably a deer or something. Satisfied with his deer theory, he pushed the incident to the back of his mind.

He parked his vehicle in its usual spot and turned off the ignition, the rumble of the engine subsiding, the sound making way for the tinny drumbeat of the raindrops on the metallic exterior. Leaping from the vehicle, he rushed around to the rear to grab his bags. Once he had his belongings in hand, he locked his car and trotted across the empty space between where he had parked and the house, wanting to get out of the miserable weather as soon as possible.

Reaching the front door, he awkwardly fumbled around for the house keys, not wanting to put his bags down on the damp, muddy ground. Finally sorting himself out, he bundled through the front door with difficulty. He was greeted by the sound of the kettle whistling on the stove and, throwing the bags on the floor, he made his way through to the kitchen.

'Great timing' Sara exclaimed jovially. 'Would you like a cup of tea?'

Michael removed his rain soaked jacket, placed it on the back of one of the dining table chairs and slumped down in the seat.

'I could murder one' he responded.

He watched admiringly as Sara set about preparing two mugs of hot tea, she really was a beauty. Her thick, blonde hair tumbled down her back and reached her waist, even without seeing a hairdresser for three years it looked stunning. She turned and sauntered towards him clutching the two mugs of tea and he watched ardently. She was like an angel, her skin flawless and smooth, her green eyes shimmered like two precious emeralds and as she approached she smiled at him, flashing a set of perfect, white teeth that glistened in the kitchen light. Somehow she had maintained her athletic physique, despite being locked up most of the time, and he admired her shapliness. If she agreed to a new start, perhaps he would allow her to start running again.

Placing one of the mugs in front of him, she took her place in the remaining seat and he snapped out of his stupor. Picking up the beverage immediately, he lifted it to his lips and gently blew across the scolding liquid before taking a tentative sip. He winced as the drink burned his lips and Sara giggled at the grimace that had spread across his face.

'I have an idea' he said suddenly. 'I think it's a really good one.'

'Okay' Sara responded, sitting forward in her seat and resting her arms on the table. 'Let's hear it.'

Shifting around in his seat, he stalled for a moment, trying to figure out how to begin. He had blurted that out with no real plan of what he was going to say. Despite his nervousness, he figured the best approach was just to rip the plaster off.

'I think we should get away from here... for good. Go somewhere new and start afresh.' He paused briefly to let his opening statement sink in, her expression unchanging. 'I just don't think it's safe for us to be around here anymore and a new start, a new life could make us truly happy. We could live a normal life, you could run again, we could explore together. Somewhere quiet and remote where we won't be known. I could sell both my residences which would give us more than enough money to live on and we wouldn't have to worry anymore.'

He had babbled at a frantic speed and allowed her a few moments to digest the word vomit. She sat perfectly still, silent and thoughtful. After what felt like an eternity he prompted a response.

'So... what do you think?'

● ● ●

Sara sat across from Michael with a kind smile planted on her face, trying to absorb this sudden suggestion of disappearing off into the sunset with the man who had ripped her away from her old life. She had accepted this as her life as a means of survival and had even grown to enjoy his company but willingly starting a life somewhere with him was something else entirely.

She had long given up any hope of being found but the news that Michael had potentially revealed himself to the detective that had led the search for her, had left her conflicted. It had brought about a new hope of seeing her parents again, of returning to a life she once enjoyed but she felt some kind of warped loyalty to her captor, as ridiculous as that was. Part of her had actually begun to enjoy her life of solitude and she was unsure if she was prepared to give it up. Even if she did, would she even be able to return to normal life? The thought was scary.

Aware that Michael's gaze was firmly fixed on her, she knew she had to respond quickly and positively, any resistance to an idea he was clearly excited about could lead to him erupting like a volcano.

'I think that sounds wonderful' she declared, managing to disguise the trepidation and confusion in her voice. 'But we definitely need to discuss it in depth, this may not be easy.'

Michael's face had lit up and she relaxed, content that she had satisfied him for now. But she needed to buy herself some time to really assess everything.

'Why don't we head upstairs, chill out and talk about it some more?' she suggested, attempting to create herself a brief moment to think about it all. Michael jumped at the opportunity and hurriedly washed up their two mugs before grabbing her hand and leading her from the kitchen. He grabbed the two bags he had thrown on the floor on his way past and dragged her up the stairs.

Once in the comfort of her room, Sara sat on her bed and Michael sat on a chair across the room. He was chattering away and she tuned in from time to time, offering up generic responses while she tried weighing the situation up in her head. She needed more time, being put on the spot in this manner was definitely not ideal.

Quarter of an hour passed while Michael excitedly talked about possible locations and how quickly they could get it all done. Sara sat on her bed, overwhelmed by the whole situation, her mind working overtime to try and work out a solution as well as be somewhat alert to him talking at her.

Suddenly the bedroom door burst open. The first thing she clocked was the look of shock and horror on Michael's face as he saw the intruder first. Sara snapped round quickly, startled by this sudden occurrence and looked straight into the eyes of Scott Harris.

CHAPTER 38

Scott stood in the doorway of the bedroom, his body rigid with shock, only his eyes moving as they attempted to rapidly take on the scene that was in front of him. He had fooled himself, thinking he was mentally prepared for whatever he found when opened the door, how wrong he was. He was dumbfounded, surprised and astonished; Sara, alive and well, sat on the bed of a well-furnished room staring straight at him – he had been right all along! Across the room from her, on an individual chair, was the man who had taken her; the man Scott was going to take to apprehend.

His eyes locked on to the face of the man who had caused so much misery and heartache, it didn't look like the face of an evil man, he looked timid and frightened. Regardless, he had been the one to cause it all, he had ruined an entire family – Sara's parents had never been the same; he had also inadvertently destroyed Scott's entire career and left his life in tatters.

Scott could feel the fury building inside of him, an intense, burning anger that raged like an unstoppable inferno. A rage that had been building inside of him for years was finally bubbling to the surface. His hands were shaking from the overwhelming surge of emotion and he clenched his fists tightly, his fingernails cutting into the skin on his palms.

Michael sat unmoving on his chair, returning the former detective's stare. Scott could see the horror on his face, the realisation that he had been caught redhanded and it was over. Not a word had been uttered, the tension was tangible, each of them waiting for the other to make a move.

It was Michael who blinked first, his gaze dropping from Scott and looking beyond the former detective and out into the dark hallway, to freedom. As if reading Michael's mind, Scott took the smallest of steps towards his target, ready for what was to come. Michael lunged toward the door but Scott was prepared and as his adversary attempted to shove him out of the way and make a run for it, he met him with a body-shuddering tackle. The two men plunged to the floor, their combined weight slamming to the ground causing the entire room to rattle.

Sara watched wide-eyed, frightened as the two men grappled on the floor right in front of her. She shuffled herself backwards on her bed, pinning herself against the wall in the corner of the room, unsure of what to do.

The battle on the bedroom floor was growing more intense, each man fighting to gain the upper hand like two stags rutting. They rolled around on the floor, grabbing at each other, each one attempting to restrain the other and avoid losing the brawl. They lurched around the room, tumbling into the walls, into the furniture, trashing the place. Finally Scott managed to get on top and he threw a punch into Michael's ribs, the villain yelping in pain as the larger man's fist connected flush with the side of his body. Sensing he was gaining the advantage, Scott pulled his fist back a second time but Michael managed to wriggle his narrow frame free. Managing to create a little separation, he pulled his leg up into chest and propelled a well-aimed kick into Scott's gut with as much force as he could muster. It did the trick and Scott doubled over, clutching his stomach and wheezing for breath. Michael saw an opportunity and leapt to his feet, trying once more to run from the room.

Scott, still struggling to catch his breath, wasn't about to give in and as his foe swept past him he reached out and grabbed his ankle. Pulling his leg out from under him, he watched as the ungainly man lost his balance and plummeted to the ground, his chin connecting loudly with the floorboards making a sickening crunch. Michael lay on his front, dazed and exhausted, his chin burning white hot with pain, blood pouring from the fresh wound. Scott, his body still heaving from being winded, shuffled over to the prone man and pinned his arms behind his back. Michael made one last effort to break free but Scott grabbed the back of his head and slammed his face into the floor, breaking his nose on impact.

Defeated, bloodied and beaten, Michael succumbed as Scott restrained him once more. Scott, victorious, allowed himself a moment to catch his breath before habitually beginning to recite the culprit his rights.

'Michael Thompson, you are under arrest for the kidnapping and unlawful captivity of Sara Williams. You do not have to say-' Scott stopped. A sudden, unbearable pain soared through the right-hand side of his body, A hot, piercing sensation that took his breath away once more. Clutching at the area with his left hand, he could feel the recognisable warm, sticky texture of blood. Pulling his hand away, he stared down at his palm which was soaked in the unmistakable crimson and slumped against the wall. He had been stabbed.

CHAPTER 39

Sara watched on, scared and horrified, as the two men battled viciously on the bedroom floor. The fight grew more intense as each man desperately tried to gain the upper hand, each one knowing that if they gave in, the result for them could be catastrophic. Sara hadn't had much time to process what had just unfolded in front of her and she was glued to her spot on the bed, unable to move, trying to get her head around the action that was taking place right in front of her.

This was the moment she had been waiting for, the moment she had yearned for. Years she had been here, confined to this one building, chaperoned on every woodland walk, all usual freedoms taken from her and she had finally been found. Long ago she had given up any hope of being rescued, of being able to return to a normal life, and see her parents again. Now, the detective who had been searching for her was right there in front of her and this was her chance at freedom. She could only assume more police would be arriving soon, he couldn't be here alone.

As the struggle raged on, she cautiously stood up and slowly vacated the room, as quiet as a church mouse. Sara moved so silently, she could have been floating and, once she reached the hallway, she relaxed. Her pulse had quickened, her breathing heavy but she had made it out of the room undetected, she wouldn't have long, however, it would only be a matter of time before one of the men noticed.

Standing at the top of the staircase, she allowed herself a moment to gather her bearings as she stared down into the dimly lit hallway. Inhaling deeply, she began her descent towards the door that led to her liberation, the fight between her captor and rescuer continuing loudly in her bedroom. She was careful and remained quiet, even though she was certain that with all the commotion they wouldn't notice her leaving anyway.

Reaching downstairs, she crept to the front door and reached out towards the door knob, her hand shaking violently – she was nervous, this was it. Grasping the cool brass with a sweaty palm, she turned the knob and swung the door open. Cold, damp air streamed in causing her to shiver, she was not dressed for the elements. However, it wasn't the icy air that shocked her, it was the fact that she was looking out into a barren opening. She thought this place would have been swarming with police by now but there was no one, she was merely greeted by the sound of the wind swirling around the desolate woodland.

Taking a hesitant step outside, she paused. Where would she go? How would she get away? She had absolutely no idea where she was. It was scary, terrifying in fact, was she even ready to go back to a normal life? She tried taking another step but it was as if an invisible force was holding her back and she stepped back inside, closing the door behind her.

She decided she couldn't just run, and not because she didn't know where she was going to go, this was her opportunity to end this once and for all. Knowing what she had to do, she stormed determinedly into the kitchen. Her mind was made up, this was her chance and she wasn't going to let it slip through her fingers. Opening one of the drawers, she selected a sharp kitchen knife and picked it up, the blade glinting in the artificial kitchen light. Turning on her heel she headed for the stairs, grasping the handle of the knife so tight that her knuckles were turning white.

Her ascent of the staircase was markedly different to her descent, her walk was swift, purposeful and unwavering. Her mind was made up and she was going to see it through.

Reaching the staircase summit, she stopped abruptly in her tracks as she heard an almighty thud. Gingerly, she inched forward and peered into the room; Michael was face down, blood pouring from his chin with the detective straddling his back. She watched as her captor tried to struggle free but the detective grabbed the back of his head and violently slammed his face into the floor, the crunching of Michael's nose breaking making her grimace.

Stepping into the doorway she stared and listened as the detective began reciting the 'right to silence' to Michael. This was her moment, she drew back the knife, looking down at her captor as she did so and an odd feeling of pity came over her. Focussing on her spot, she slammed the knife into the man's side, the blade comfortably slicing through the flesh and she yanked it back out.

Shocked at her own actions, she turned and threw up in the hallway. Turning back to the room she watched as the result of her act unfolded. The detective, the man who had come to rescue her, was slumped against the wall, clutching at the injury she had inflicted. A dazed, battered and confused Michael stared up at her, covered in blood, his mouth gaping.

'What did you do?' he asked, flabbergasted.

'I did... I did what I had to.' she said quietly. 'Now get up, we have to go.'

Helping him up, she supported his weight and guided him down the stairs, leaving the detective to bleed out alone.

CHAPTER 40

Clutching at the puncture wound in the side of his body, Scott desperately tried to stem the bleeding. He had already lost a lot of blood and no matter how much pressure he applied, the blood still gushed between his fingers. His shirt was saturated with the claret liquid, some of it drying and giving off a brownish hue. A crimson pool had collected on the floor around him and it slowly crept across the old floorboards, as more blood gushed from the slashed flesh, expanding the puddle.

His breathing had become shallow and more rapid as his heart worked overtime to try and keep him alive, sweat streamed from his pores and he could taste the salty fluid on his lips. He was beginning to shake and he knew that he was going into shock but he had to try and remain composed, survival mode had kicked in.

Reaching out he grasped at the bed sheet with a quivering hand, frantically trying to find something more effective to stem the flow. He leaned toward the bed and groaned loudly, even a movement as simple as this left him in agony, a sharp, searing pain surged down the left hand side of his body where the knife wound was. Yanking hard with the limited strength he had remaining, he pulled the bed sheet free and immediately pressed it to his injury, wincing in pain as he did so.

Scott was beginning to feel faint and light headed, he knew his condition was deteriorating rapidly and he drastically needed help. If only he had just left this alone, if only he had continued with his life and found a new job, he wouldn't be here on the floor of a dusty old house, close to death. But that wasn't him, who would he have been if he had just given up, when he knew deep down she was still alive? It would have made him question his entire identity and he was glad he had tried, even if it looked increasingly likely it was going to lead to his premature death. Even during this moment of peril the irony wasn't lost on him. This job had been his life, a life he had wasted because of his love for his profession and now it was going to be the end of him.

He still hadn't wrapped his head around the fact that it was Sara who had stabbed him, the girl he was trying to rescue had plunged the knife into the soft flesh on his side, just below his rib cage. Three years in captivity, three years with just that lunatic for company had clearly left her a little unstable and he wasn't surprised by that. Obviously he had expected a completely different reaction but three years was a long time to manipulate someone, to brainwash someone.

Pulling his mobile phone from his pocket, he was going to give it one last roll of the dice. If he was going to die here, he didn't want it to be in vain, it had to be worth it. He wasn't going to give up until he had taken his final breath. Opening the 'maps' application on his phone, he shared his location with his former colleague, James Lock, before calling him. The phone rang for what seemed like an eternity, seconds felt like minutes and then it cut off. Scott closed his eyes in frustration, he had to make this call. Redialling, he prayed that Lock would answer this time, it was his last opportunity to save the girl. The ring tone buzzed again for a painfully long time and just as he was about to give up, the phone was answered.

'Scott? Why the fu-' Scott cut him off.

'James... just listen... carefully. You have to listen carefully.' Even talking had become an effort for the injured detective. 'I have... just shared my location with you. I've... I've found the girl... she's alive. I'm really hurt but I have found her... I have found Sara, she's alive!'

'Scott what are y-' James was cut off again.

'Look mate... just get here... get everyone here. Michael has taken her, they're... on the run... and I need a paramedic, I've been stabbed. Please... just hurry.' Scott hung up.

Dropping his phone to the floor, he relaxed, he had done what he could. If his last act was getting the help needed to get that girl back to her parents, her loving family, he could die happy. Scott's breathing had become even more erratic, he was beginning to hyperventilate. His heart rate was slowing and his eyelids were getting heavy. Knowing that if he didn't stay awake, he may never wake up, he valiantly battled the urge to close his eyes. The fight became increasingly difficult as time wore on and he lost the strength to continue. Slowly slumping to his side, he ended up lying in the puddle of his own blood. He gazed across the shimmering red pool, wishing he had the strength to carry on but it was out of his hands now. Eventually he succumbed, let his eyes close and slipped into unconsciousness.

• • •

Detective Constable Lock was trying to digest what he had just heard. Scott had found Sara? She was actually alive? He had been right all along.

It was late but he leapt up out of bed immediately and began making calls. He had gotten the location from Scott and he was about to send the cavalry in, he was going to throw every man and woman he could at that area, plus the kitchen sink.

It took him a few minutes to get everything in motion and he worked at a frantic pace. He had the police from the area heading out immediately and his own officers heading there as well, along with aerial help from the helicopter. Paramedics were also on their way to the address and hopefully they would be able to save Scott before it was too late. This whole situation had unfolded so suddenly and the adrenaline coursed through his body.

Rushing around his bedroom he hurriedly threw on an outfit, not really paying attention to the ensemble he was piecing together. It didn't really matter, he just needed to get on the road as soon as he could and get there. Once he was ready, he grabbed his phone and called his superintendent as he headed towards the stairs. As he made his way down the staircase, his superior answered and Lock immediately began giving him an update on what had happened.

'So I've had a call from Scott Harris, he's found the girl... alive! The suspect has made off with the girl and Scott has been badly hurt but he managed to send me the location. I've sent everyone, boss, including the chopper. We're finally going to nail this scumbag.' Lock stopped, waiting for the inevitable praise for orchestrating the operation so swiftly but he was to be bitterly disappointed.

'Lock, what on earth are you doing? Scott is a waste of time, a loose cannon whose best days are behind him. You cannot trust the word of that man! This is going to be a wild goose chase, an absolute waste of time, money and resources!' Nick was livid, Lock could hear his voice shaking.

James was dumbfounded, he couldn't believe this was the reaction he was getting. He was silent for a moment, staring silently at the phone that he had removed from his ear, a disbelieving expression on his tired face. Raising the phone back to his ear, he cleared his throat, licked his lips and responded.

'With all due respect, Sir… fuck you.' With that, Lock promptly hung up and he was on the road.

CHAPTER 41

Grasping the steering wheel tightly in his slender, bony hands, Michael was breathing heavily. Drenched in his own blood, which was drying rapidly on his skin causing an uncomfortable, sticky sensation, he was exhausted. The altercation with the determined former detective had left him reeling and he allowed himself a brief moment to catch his breath and calm down. Sara sat alongside him in the stationary vehicle, still clutching the blood-soaked blade in her right hand.

Michael couldn't believe she had come to his aid in the manner she did but he was grateful for it. The sight of her standing over them after she had plunged the knife into Scott Harris' side both excited and terrified him. She had saved him from being arrested, at least for now, but she would also be wanted after that act. He had to get them away from there and fast.

Rain had begun to smatter the windscreen, each delicate drop making a timid thud on the glass. In normal circumstances, the noise would've been soothing, almost therapeutic but it wasn't something they had time to enjoy. The wind and rain increased as they sat, unmoving, outside the house. The raindrops, that fell gently just moments earlier, became thick and heavy and hammered down upon his vehicle, the resonance sounding like hundreds of miniscule battering rams trying to force their way inside the safety of the 4x4. Powerful gusts of wind rocked the vehicle, slamming repeatedly into the side of them, unrelenting. The trees that towered overhead, swayed violently in the swirling gale; the same trees that always made him feel so protected, so hidden, now did nothing to assuage his internal terror.

Suddenly Sara's voice broke through his stupor and she yelled at him, her voice frantic and frightened.

'Michael, what are you doing? Get us away from here now... *please!*' Her voice shook with fear as she made her request and he snapped out of his daydream.

Turning the key in the ignition, his car fired into life and he pressed his foot on the accelerator, the tyres spinning on the rain-soaked ground. Turning onto the beaten track, that would lead them to their freedom, he abandoned his usual cautious approach and put his foot down. His vehicle rocked around turbulently as he drove over each bump and through each dip, the off-road tyres churning up the wet dirt, sending a muddy spray firing out behind them.

The headlights lit up the track in front of them, illuminating the torrential downpour and bathing the trees that ran along the edge of the track in artificial light. The darkness that surrounded them felt intimidating for the first time, the woodland that was once their natural wall, their protector, would soon be overrun with police and he didn't want to be there for it, they couldn't be there for it.

Stopping abruptly at the end of the track, he looked both ways on the road. It was deserted, hauntingly so, the only sounds were the car engine and the rain that continued to thunder down on the exterior of the vehicle and the tarmac in front of them. Keeping his wits about him, he cautiously began to pull out and turn right, when his eyes caught something in the distance. Staring hard through the downpour and the darkness, he could make out the faint glow of flashing, blue light. 'THE POLICE!' Michael yelled and aborted his right turn in favour of the opposite direction.

As he turned left, he slammed his foot to the floor and accelerated hard, the wheels of the off-road vehicle spinning up hard on the rain-soaked tarmac before finally gaining traction. Glancing across at Sara, who still held the knife tightly, he could see the terror etched across her face and prayed that he would be able to get them out of this situation. Glancing in his rear-view mirror he could still see the distant blue light that heralded the approach of the emergency services and a knot developed in his stomach. His own need to be near the detective and satiate his thirst for attention had brought the entire investigation crashing down on their heads. This was entirely his fault.

Driving with purpose through the increasingly stormy weather, he desperately tried to create distance between themselves and the police that were rolling in. After several minutes, he took another look in his rear-view mirror and was greeted with nothing but darkness. He relaxed a little and slowed the vehicle to a more controlled pace, it seemed they had gotten away.

From the corner of his eye he took another peek at the knife safely grasped in Sara's hand and then looked at her face. She was rigid, her eyes wide and staring straight ahead, unblinking. He was worried about her but he also wanted to know why she had stabbed the detective. Although he was aware she had gotten used to her new life, he always figured that if she was confronted with an opportunity to return to her old life, she would reach out and grab it with both hands.

Tentatively he reached out and placed his hand on Sara's leg, she glanced at it but didn't flinch or swat him away which made him smile. He just wanted to sooth her, reassure her and talk to her.

'Little Lamb? Are you okay?' he asked softly.

She turned and looked at him, staring directly into his eyes and pushed his hand off of her thigh. Her gaze was cold and empty, her expression haunted and her face gaunt. Her stare didn't drop from his face, even when he turned back to focus on the road in front of him. The question he had asked, seemed as though it dangled in the air between them, remaining unanswered. In hindsight, it was probably a stupid and insensitive question and the tension was palpable.

After what felt like an age, he heard her take a deep breath and she dropped the stare that had been burning into the side of his head for several minutes. Finally she answered.

'Am I okay? AM I OKAY?' she raised her voice. 'No, I am not fucking okay, Michael. This whole situation is awful. I'm scared, I'm confused and I may have just killed a man who was only trying to help me. Did you really think I would be okay right now?' Sara was shaking with suppressed anger and he was suddenly nervous about the weapon that she still held tightly in her white-knuckled hand.

It was his turn to be quiet before attempting to reply to the verbal onslaught that just tumbled from her lips. For the first time in their 'relationship', he was the one who was frightened and it was a feeling he didn't appreciate. He thought long and hard before answering, not wanting to antagonise her further and he could once again feel her stare locked on him while he pondered.

Opening his mouth to speak, he stopped and the words caught in his throat. He was distracted by the sudden appearance of more blue lights, this time in front of them. His heart sank, the knot in his stomach tightened and he felt sick. This was it, there was nowhere to turn.

Sara, still staring at him, her brow furrowed and her fury bubbling away inside of her, saw the look of defeat descend on Michael's angular face. Turning to face forward, she was greeted by the same blue glow that he was currently gawping at and she panicked, she did not want to go to prison. Stifling the anxiousness, she decided she was going to take the initiative and get them out of this.

'Look, Michael, just stay calm and drive normally.' she said it softly, calmly. 'If they're heading to the house, hopefully they'll just drive straight past. Just stay calm and don't give them any reason to stop.'

He nodded but he was anything but calm. Sweating profusely, he tightened his grip on the steering wheel and stuck to the speed limit. He could feel his heart hammering inside his rib cage and one of his legs was shaking nervously. The blue glow had grown, signifying the rapidly decreasing distance between them and it wasn't long before the headlights of the oncoming vehicles loomed into view. Michael's pulse was racing, his breathing erratic and shallow, he had never been this scared.

With his gaze firmly locked on the vehicles in the distance that were approaching at speed, he concentrated hard on his driving. Nice and steady, calm and easy, just let them drive past. Before he knew it, the police cars were right in front of them. The first one whizzed past in a blur of vibrant blue light, the siren blaring loudly. It was closely followed by a second car, a third and a fourth. He kept his cool and maintained a steady speed as he watched the police cars drive out of site in the rear-view mirror.

Exhaling loudly, he relaxed, as did Sara. They had done it, they were in the clear now and Michael was going to make sure he used this window of opportunity to get them far away from here for good. Sara was smiling and visibly relaxing which made him relax, in turn. It seemed that for now, they were safe.

'Yes! We did it!' Michael yelled suddenly, smacking the steering wheel with an open palm. 'We just need to find somewhere we can lie low for a day or two.'

Sara, still grinning, responded softly. 'Anywhere… anywhere will do. Just get us away from here.'

Michael smiled and nodded before flicking the radio on so they had some music to listen to as they continued their journey. Elated, Michael tapped along with the music, using the steering will as a makeshift drum and relaxed fully now they were finally away from the police presence.

Suddenly, another sound caught his attention and he switched the radio off. Confused, Sara went to object but he held up a hand to silence her swiftly. 'Listen!' he whispered. Listening intently, Michael tried to figure out what the sound was but could only decipher a gentle chugging from an origin he couldn't determine. Sara could hear it as well and both of them were looking around frantically, trying to identify the source of this unknown sound. The volume was increasing, the chug growing louder and louder, yet all they could see was the rain-soaked road ahead of them. Before they were able to figure it out themselves, the noise had become deafening and the source apparent – a police helicopter. Suddenly they had been lit up by the helicopter's huge spotlight and they had been found.

Michael, once again, slammed his foot on the accelerator and roared off into the night, hoping to shake off the law enforcement aircraft. The roads were treacherous from the ongoing downpour and each sharp turn made the 4x4 slide on the wet surface. Sara was gripping her seat tightly with one hand, trying to not get thrown about, her other hand was still firmly gripping on to the knife.

Glancing over his shoulder, Michael could see the helicopter hot on their tail and had no idea how he would manage to lose them. To make matters worse, he could also see the familiar blue lights behind them which meant the police cars would soon be joining the chase. The panic grew inside him once again, the feeling of peace from mere seconds earlier was gone, he couldn't see a way out now and the thought terrified him.

Before long, several police cars were right behind him, the exact number of vehicles he didn't know and the helicopter still soared overhead in the dark night sky. One of the police cars suddenly made an aggressive approach down his right flank but he blocked the attack, he knew they would run him off the road if they got the opportunity. The chase was reaching perilous speeds and he was no longer heading in any particular direction, he was just trying to shake off his pursuers. Veering round a corner at high speed and in the wrong lane, he came face to face with another police car. Swerving harshly to try and avoid what would likely be a fatal collision, he narrowly missed the oncoming vehicle but his rear end clipped the front of the police car and sent them both spiralling out of control.

Michael's vehicle spun to a halt in the middle of the road, facing the opposite direction to which he was originally headed, both Sara and himself unhurt. The police car wasn't so lucky; the leader of the chasing pack hadn't been able to avoid their out of control colleague and had slammed into them at speed, the sickening sound of twisted metal echoing in the surrounding woodland and both vehicles ended up blocking the road.

Seizing his opportunity, Michael made to drive off but his vehicle felt heavy and slow and struggled to pull away. As he managed to slowly build up some sort of speed he could feel the drag caused by a flat tyre – there was no way he would be able to lose the chopper in this state.

'There! Over there!' Sara's frantic tone pierced the air and she was gesturing wildly to a narrow track just off the main road. 'Pull in there, we can hide!'

The track she pointed at was overgrown with out of control vegetation and mature oak trees towered overhead, their canopies reaching out towards each other creating a natural shelter. It might just be enough to get out of sight of the helicopter. Pulling into the sheltered track, he stopped and switched off the engine.

'Let's go.' he said to Sara. 'We can get away on foot.' An obvious act of desperation but with that they both exited the damaged vehicle and began their trudge into the night.

CHAPTER 42

Driving with purpose through the incessant rainfall, siren bellowing and blue lights flashing behind the grill of his Audi, adrenaline coursed through Detective Sergeant Lock's body. The torrent was lashing down outside, the wind strengthening the precipitation's power and his windscreen wipers were working tirelessly to keep his vision clear. Despite the dangerous driving conditions, his approach was unwavering and the excitement and apprehension grew as he journeyed towards his destination.

The roads were relatively clear, the few vehicles he did come across pulled out of the way quickly to create a path that he navigated smoothly. This was no time for dithering, no time for hesitation, not only was he close to being able to close one of the most notorious cases he had worked on, but his old friend and colleague needed his help.

He had just received word, via radio, that several patrol cars and the paramedics were almost at the scene, and he wouldn't be far behind, he just hoped they would get there in time to save his friend's life. As he turned on to a dark and secluded stretch of road, his sat-nav came to life and alerted him that he was merely minutes from arriving at his intended location. Despite the fact that he knew he was close, as he took in his surroundings, he was shocked that there could be any buildings here at all. The road was narrow and without any source of light, besides his headlights, the area seemed bleak and devoid of any life. All he could see were never-ending rows of large pine trees, standing like soldiers in the darkness.

As he continued his approach, he could see the flashing blue lights of emergency service vehicles lighting up the dark sky like a homing beacon. His police radio was keeping him continually updated with the movements of the officers he had deployed and it announced the arrival of several of them at the house, along with an ambulance. Just moments later, he had pulled up outside the house alongside them and hastily made to vacate his vehicle and get to his friend in need. However, a sudden commotion on his radio stopped him in his tracks.

'We have a visual on the suspect's vehicle. Air support in pursuit, we need ground support. Four incident response vehicles just drove past, we need you to turn around immediately.' Suddenly the radio was filled with chatter from the four vehicles confirming they had heard the request and that they would be on their way and would be joining the pursuit.

Lock paused and listened for a moment, gazed up at the house, and hesitated. He came to the conclusion that his friend was in the best hands, with the paramedics, and there was nothing he could do. He got back in his vehicle and decided to join the pursuit

Grabbing his radio, he yelled into it. 'This is Detective Sergeant James Lock, please share your location, I am on my way.' He paused and waited for a response and through the static, got a swift reply.

'Suspect is heading west, at speed. I repeat, the suspect is heading west.'

Pulling a U-turn on the wet ground, James navigated the uneven track he had only just driven down and turned left onto the road, heading in the direction of where the suspect was fleeing. Slamming his foot on the accelerator, his vehicle gripped the saturated tarmac and roared into life, the force pinning him back into his seat.

Determinedly and unfaltering, he soared down the road through the driving rain, reaching dangerous speeds – there wasn't a chance in hell he was letting Michael Thompson get away. This was it, this was their opportunity, with the helicopter on him and several police cars on their way, there was no way out and James couldn't wait to arrest the scumbag.

Up ahead of him in the distance, he could once again see blue lights flashing and the spotlight from the helicopter was visible – he was close. Suddenly, his radio crackled into life again and a frantic, panicked voice broke the silence.

'We need paramedics immediately! We've had a collision between two of our patrol cars, send an ambulance now! The road is blocked, air support will remain in pursuit!'

James was approaching the scene of the accident, slowing down before coming to a gentle halt a short distance away from the chaos and he couldn't believe what was unfolding in front of him. It was pure mayhem, one of the patrol cars had slammed into the side of another, causing it to buckle. A third had rammed into the back of his colleague and the front end had caved in, the carnage fully blocking the road. The remaining two cars had managed to avoid the pile up and the officers were out trying to help their colleagues. The suspect was long gone, with the helicopter still in pursuit.

Leaping out of his vehicle, Lock ran toward the mangled vehicles, the wind and rain battering him as he advanced. The sight that greeted him wasn't a pleasant one; one officer lay on the ground, bloodied and struggling to breathe while a colleague tried helping her, two further officers sat on the saturated floor nursing injuries. The unfortunate driver and passenger of the vehicle that collided with the side of the oncoming patrol car both remained in their vehicle, alive but badly hurt. The driver of the buckled vehicle was slumped in his seat, unmoving and another officer was attempting to help them but Lock watched on helplessly as that officer turned away and confirmed the death of the driver.

The scene that was unfolding in front of him was one of pure devastation; five injured officers, three of them seriously hurt and one who had lost his life. The suspect no doubt using this time to create some separation. Paramedics were quickly on the scene and began attending to the injured officers. Lock signalled to the remaining officers from the two vehicles that hadn't been involved in the impacts and they jogged over to him.

'You guys good to continue? He's close and we can't let him get away.'

'Yes, Sarge' one responded, the others nodded in agreement.

'Good, let's go. We're no use here anyway.' he gestured to a gap around the edge of the accident. 'We'll drive around there, on the grass. Let's go and get this piece of shit!'

Climbing back into his vehicle, he cautiously navigated around the collision, the two remaining patrol vehicles following closely and they continued the chase. Radioing through to the chopper, Lock asked for a location but was answered with another frantic response.

'Suspect on foot, I repeat, suspect on foot! Get the dogs here!'

Lock smiled, they were on foot? They had him now, there was no way out.

CHAPTER 43

Traversing the treacherous terrain of the track that led to the house, two ambulances and two police patrol cars pulled up outside of the run-down building. The rain continued to hammer down around them and the tyres of their vehicles slid to a halt on the saturated ground.

Not wasting any time, the four paramedics had gathered their equipment and vacated their vehicles, the heavy bags they carried making each stride more perilous on the rain-soaked dirt, their boots making a satisfying squelch with each step they took.

Reaching the entrance to the dilapidated building, they were greeted by the four officers that had arrived with them. They had all been briefed on what to expect so there was no hesitation, no dithering – time was of the essence if they were going to save the former detective. The officers entered first, two of them breaking off to ensure the downstairs was secure, the other two led the medical personnel up the stairs. They made their ascent swiftly but cautiously, keeping their wits about them.

Light streamed out from the room they were heading to and illuminated the hallway they were approaching. The officers paused at the doorway, allowing the paramedics to head into the room first and the sight they were greeted with was one of pure bedlam. The room was trashed, the scene of an obvious struggle; furniture was knocked over and broken, various items littered the floor and there were smears of blood on every surface imaginable. Lying in the midst of all the chaos, in a pool of his own blood was Scott Harris, prone and unmoving.

The four paramedics set about their work immediately, three of them dropping to their knees and unpacking their bags, removing the various pieces of equipment they would need to try and save the stricken detective, while the fourth grabbed Scott's wrist to check his pulse.

'We have a pulse!' they confirmed. 'It's weak but we have a pulse!'

'He's lost an awful lot of blood!' one of the other paramedics stated. 'We have to get him to the hospital, ASAP.'

Turning to the two police officers who were still standing in the doorway, one of the paramedics asked if they could assist by getting a stretcher from one of the ambulances. After a brief explanation of where to find it, the two officers duly obliged and rushed downstairs while the paramedics continued to do what they could to keep the mortally wounded detective from slipping into the clutches of death. The paramedic who was dealing with the wound had managed to successfully stop the bleeding and another had applied a manual resuscitator to keep Scott's lungs working – it was all hands on deck.

Outside, the two officers were hastily retrieving the stretcher from the back of one of the ambulances and were having to battle the rapidly worsening weather conditions; the rain was unrelenting and strong gusts of wind burst into the clearing, almost knocking them from their feet. A distant rumble of thunder roared in the darkness, like a lion about to battle a rival. Finally freeing up the stretcher, the two officers eagerly ran it back into the building with difficulty, still toiling against the conditions.

Rushing past their colleagues who stood guard at the entrance, they finally reached the sanctuary of the building and launched up the flight of stairs with the stretcher. The paramedics were ready and waiting and the officers placed the stretcher on the floor next to their colleague and stood back while the team of paramedics carefully shifted the limp, almost lifeless body of the detective onto the stretcher.

While two paramedics lifted the stretcher from the floor, as gently as possible, the other two carried all the equipment, assisted by the police officers. They carefully navigated the staircase, that was damp from their footfall, and headed outside into the increasingly stormy conditions. They moved as quickly as they could and got the detective into the back of one of the ambulances, hooking him up to the heart monitor and getting on their way. One of the paramedics drove the other ambulance on his own so two of them could remain with the detective in the ambulance that was transporting him.

Sirens blaring, they sped down the road in the direction of the hospital, the gentle beeping of the monitor that signified the beating of Scott's heart resounding in the back of the vehicle. One of the paramedics was on the phone ensuring that the hospital was ready and awaiting the arrival of the injured man,

'We have a forty-one year old male with a single stab wound just below the rib cage and a dangerous amount of blood loss. Pulse is weak and blood pressure is low-' Suddenly the paramedic was interrupted by the sound of the heart monitor emitting a loud, continuous, shrill beep – Scott's heartbeat had stopped!

The paramedics leapt into action to try and save him in unison, their movements synchronised and efficient. While one of them cut his shirt off to ensure his chest was clear, the other grabbed and applied the defibrillator. The familiar sound of the power ramping up filled the air and when it was ready the paramedic yelled 'CLEAR!' and pushed the buttons, sending an electrical pulse coursing through Scott's body. He jolted from the force of the shock but the continuous beep held strong and the paramedic prepared for a second attempt. 'CLEAR!' Nothing. The high-pitched, ear-splitting beep persisted and the paramedic yelled out in frustration. 'We're losing him!'

Deciding to go in for a third attempt, yelling 'CLEAR' a third time and applying the electrical pulse once more. *Beep... beep... beep... beep.* Finally his heart had started again. The paramedic sat back flustered with sweat on his brow and his breathing heavy, his colleague placed a reassuring hand on his shoulder. Allowing his colleague a moment to catch his breath, he leaned through to the front and spoke to the driver.

'Step on it, mate. We need to get him to the hospital fast.'

CHAPTER 44

Running hand in hand, Michael and Sara desperately tried to escape the view of the helicopter that was hunting them from the sky. Despite the protective arms of the large trees that reached out above their heads, they were unable to successfully hide from their airbourne follower.

They ran breathlessly and resolutely, determined to get away but the weather conditions were making their attempt at an escape difficult and slowed them down considerably. Torrential rain hammered down around them relentlessly; large, painful droplets that battered against their cold, saturated bodies. A heavy flow of water ran beneath their feet, tiny splashes dancing around them as the raindrops plummeted from the heavens into the expanding pools of water.

A powerful, brutal wind billowed around them, the occasional gust almost wiping them from their feet, the dense trees that reared above them were swaying back and forth, almost like a crowd urging a marathon runner towards the finish line. Each creak of the timber that strained against the strength of the gale sounded like a disappointed groan.

Despite the worsening conditions and the odds stacked against them, they weren't going to give up. Even with the helicopter on top of them, its spotlight occasionally breaking through a gap in the trees, illuminating them as a reminder of its presence, they were going to give it their all.

The countryside track they were using as their escape route was overgrown and unkempt; long, wispy branches from the out of control vegetation reached out and whipped them across their faces as they ran but they ignored the discomfort, the pain was nothing compared to how they would feel if they were captured.

All of a sudden, Sara lost her footing and fell to the floor, landing in the thick, wet mud and pools of water with a splash and in doing so, lost her grip on the knife she had been carrying since they left the house. Michael hastily made to scoop her up but she resisted while searching for the weapon.

'NO!' she yelled. 'I need to find it, I can't leave it for them to find!'

Michael was irritated by the sudden halt to their momentum but got down onto his hands and knees in the sludge and helped her look for the missing knife. After a couple of frantic moments, Sara yelped with joy as she found the blade and crawled into Michael's arms, sobbing heavily. Michael held her close while she was overcome with emotion.

The chugging of the helicopter was ear-splitting as it hovered above them, trying to pinpoint their location with the spotlight. As the light danced between the branches it was enough to partially illuminate Sara's face and he cupped his muddy hands under her chin and lifted it so their eyes met.

'We have to keep moving, my Little Lamb. We have to keep going.'

Sara nodded, grabbed his hand and they carefully stood up together to continue their attempted escape into the darkness. They were both shivering violently now, covered in freezing cold mud and soaked through to the skin. If they didn't get out of this weather soon, they may not have to worry about being captured, hypothermia would probably claim them. The track sloped down suddenly and with no light to guide their way, they navigated the terrain with great difficulty, sliding about and battling hard to stay on their feet. The trees at this part of the track had grown even more dense and the helicopter's spotlight was moving erratically trying to locate the couple.

Just as it seemed as though the track was never going to end, the trees began to dwindle and they reached an opening that led into a vast expanse of fields. Greeted by nothing other than emptiness and the daunting dark of the night, they paused, unsure of where to go. Thunder rumbled overhead, a deep, unnerving boom that startled both of them. A second rumble followed, this one louder, more dramatic and intimidating, it was as if Mother Nature herself was against them and was trying to articulate her disapproval. They stood rooted to the spot, statuesque and with no idea what to do next; if they turned back they would be heading into the eye of the storm, the thick of the fight and no doubt into the back of a police car. If they continued ahead, they would be out in the open with nowhere to hide from their aerial pursuer.

A flash of lightning suddenly filled the dark night sky with its brilliant blue radiance. The crackle that followed sounded like a witch's cackle and it echoed around them making Michael jump. Sara, however, was unmoving, her eyes drawn towards something in the distance. As a second fork of lightning ripped through the sky like an electrical trident being thrown, she got another glimpse of what she thought was a building.

'Michael, did you see that?' she asked.

'See what?' he replied, bemused.

Sara didn't answer, her eyes were still locked forward, waiting patiently for confirmation. She was rewarded as more lightning tore through the black sky, its luminescence showing her exactly what she thought she had seen – a building!

'Straight ahead, Michael! There's a building!'

The helicopter had turned back, it was low on fuel, and Sara assumed it was giving up, Michael knew different. Either way, this was their opportunity to at least try to hide – they had to make a break for the building.

'OK, on three we run and we run hard' Michael said. 'One..two… THREE!'

Still hand in hand, the two of them bolted through the field in front of them. The tall grass lapped around their legs, saturating them further, each rapid stride unsteady on the soft earth.

As they sprinted towards shelter and potential safety, it began to hail; the tiny, icy pellets pelting against them like little bullets but it did nothing to slow them down, the lure of a place to get out of the elements was too attractive. After what felt like hours they reached the building, an old, disused barn and entered, the large door creaking loudly as it swung open aided by the wind and banged against the interior wall. They rushed inside and hastily closed the door behind them, sliding the ancient, rusty bolt across to secure it.

Finally, they could take a moment to rest and they both slumped to the floor, leaning against the damp, rotten timber that made up the barn walls. The protection from the elements was welcome but the storm raged on outside, the mixture of rain and hail rattling against the roof and the entire building moaning and groaning as it battled against the mighty wind.

Sara rested her head on Michael's shoulder for a moment and he could feel her relax. He was still nervous, however, his body aching from the tension as he tried to figure out what their next move would be. They were without a vehicle, cowering in what was effectively a large shed and once the helicopter came back with its infrared camera they would be sitting ducks! They sat for a while, catching their breath and enjoying a brief moment of tranquillity. Other than the turbulent weather that continued to rage outside, it was silent, eerily silent and Sara battled the urge to sleep.

Instead, she caressed the knife that she had clung on to so desperately, although she hoped she wouldn't have to use it again, she was prepared to do whatever it took to get away. Her naivety led her to believe that there was a chance the police might just give up, thinking they had escaped but deep down she knew that was never going to happen, the police would do everything in their power to apprehend them.

The weather outside was beginning to calm down, the rain and hail had ceased and a gentle wind remained. A near silence descended over the barn where they were hiding and the quiet was welcome. However, as the wind noise lowered it exposed the distant rhythmic humming of the propeller on the returning helicopter. A lump caught in Sara's throat as the din grew louder, closer until it was right on top of them – they had been found.

The whirring propeller caused the rickety building to shudder as it hovered above and Michael and Sara huddled together, defeated. They had trapped themselves in here, effectively handing themselves over on a silver platter and there was nothing they could do about it now. As they held each other the wailing sound of police sirens became apparent, followed closely by the barking of police dogs and shouts of multiple officers as they closed in on where they were concealing themselves.

Sara was gripped by the icy hand of fear, they probably knew that she was the one who had stabbed the detective and she didn't want to go to prison. Placing a filthy, mud-covered palm on Michael's face, she turned his head so she could look at him, just about able to make out his face through the darkness.

'I love you' she whispered and pressed her lips forcefully but tenderly against his. As he responded to this show of affection and kissed her back, she took the knife she had been cradling for so long and plunged it deep into his chest, the blade piercing his heart. He pulled away from her, his eyes wide with shock and she cried as she watched the life slowly drain from his body. His mouth opened as if to say something but instead, he uttered one final, raspy breath and he was gone.

Sara screamed out in agony, a heartbreaking, piercing scream that would've chilled the bones of anyone who heard it and pulled the knife free from Michael's chest. She continued to weep as the barking dogs and police officers approached. Taking the blood-soaked knife, she gripped it tightly, pressed the blade firmly against her wrist and dragged the knife through the flesh. Her body began to shake from the shock of the sudden pain but she transferred the knife to her other hand and slashed at the other wrist in the same manner.

Dropping the knife to the floor, her arms flopped to her sides, she sat as her lifeblood gushed rapidly from the two wounds and she began to feel faint. Reaching out she grabbed Michael's cold, lifeless hand and held on to it tightly as she took her last breath.

CHAPTER 45

Pulling up alongside the abandoned vehicle that belonged to the fugitive and his hostage, Detective Sergeant James Lock stepped out of his vehicle and into the horizontal precipitation. The two patrol cars that had accompanied him parked up alongside his Audi, their blue lights flashing, dancing off the trees that surrounded them.

Lock was placing a protective police vest over his rain-soaked shirt as the uniformed officers joined him by his car. They stood silently, patiently waiting for some direction from their superior who was now pre-paring his police issue Glock 17M, his face contorted into one of pure determination and focus and his hands were shaking as he holstered the handgun.

Turning to face his hastily assembled team, the remains of the horrific accident that had occured, he could see they were all a little shell-shocked. Thanks to the continuously flashing blue lights, their facial expressions were clear and they all looked as though they had seen a ghost – an understandable reaction to witnessing a serious collision that involved their friends and colleagues.

'I know you have all been through a lot all ready tonight but we're close, too close and we have to catch this guy.' Lock paused and the officers stood stationary and silently as he looked at each one of them before continuing. 'He has critically wounded one of our own, caused a crash which has taken a friend and colleague from us, and ripped this girl away from her family and life causing endless heartache. The chopper will be back from refuelling soon and canine units are on their way. Once they're here, we're on the hunt so prepare yourselves.'

An enthusiastic chorus of 'Yes, Sarge' resounded from the four officers, they were all as determined as he was and he turned away from them to gather the last of his items, a torch and a radio. Strapping his radio to the shoulder strap of his protective vest, he called through to the channel of the helicopter.

'This is DS James Lock speaking, what is your ETA? Over.' He paused and waited for a response, which came swiftly.

'We are ten minutes out, Sarge. Over.'

As the correspondence ended, reinforcements arrived; two armed units and two canine units. Without hesitation all of the arriving officers leapt out of their vehicles and busied themselves getting prepared for what was to come and Lock watched on, satisfied with the urgency and efficiency. Two German Shepherd police dogs were barking enthusiastically, eager to get working.

They were ready, they just needed a more precise location – he wasn't about to risk leading his team into the unknown, there had been enough surprises for one evening.

Gathering all the officers, he briefed them on what their approach was going to be and they all listened intently – everyone wanted this resolved. As he wrapped up his plan of action, the welcome sound of the helicopter propeller graced his ears. Seconds later, it roared over all their heads like a metal eagle, the volume of the propeller blades tearing through the air and reverberating around them.

Lock's heart felt like it was in his throat, pounding away as if trying to escape and the familiar mixture of excitement, anxiety and dread washed over him. These moments in any case were huge but this was a different beast, this had caused so much pain, so much suffering for so long and he now had the opportunity to end it all.

Staring into the black emptiness of the track, he waited patiently for some instruction from his aerial team. Rainwater mixed with nervous sweat ran down his forehead and into his eyes, making them sting.

Wiping the moisture away with the back of his hand, he continued his unrelenting stare into the darkness.

Static from his radio broke through the silence and interrupted his stupor, one of the officers from the helicopter spoke up.

'Suspects located, I repeat, suspects located, Currently sheltered in an old barn, we will light it up with the spotlight. Move in!'

This was it, the moment Lock had been waiting for, they had them now and they could finally end this, finally return the girl to her family and to her normal life.

'Let's go!' Lock yelled. 'Dogs up front, please and keep your wits about you. This guy has eluded us for years, I can't see him going down easily!'

The officers began their march forward, the two German Shepherds straining at their leashes, panting heavily, desperate to begin the search. Multiple torches combined to light the path ahead of them and Lock and the armed units had their guns drawn ready.

The rain was heavy and mixed with hail, making the track difficult to walk on and they all worked hard to keep their footing. A gentle haze drifted in the torchlight, an accumulation of all their heavy breathing in the cold, damp air. Their approach was cautious but purposive, knowing that with each step they took they were getting closer to a resolution.

Suddenly, the two dogs started barking wildly and pulled harshly against their leashes, the two handlers practically being dragged forwards – the canines had latched on to a scent. The weather was calming, the rain and hail ceasing but the wind continued to whip between the trees and swirl around them. The steady chug of the helicopter propeller was apparent as the weather eased off and became clearer as they got closer to their destination.

Reaching the end of the track, where the trees stopped, they looked out into the open field and on the opposite side their aerial support hovered with their powerful spotlight trained firmly on the old barn, illuminating it for all to see. They began their final stretch of the journey, the pace quicker now they could see their goal and the dogs were becoming increasingly excitable.

Traipsing through the long grass, their feet sinking into the saturated earth, it took what felt like an eternity to reach the old barn. The downwash caused by the propeller was spraying them with wet mud but they powered through, unaffected, determined to reach their target swiftly.

Lock used hand signals to direct his team to surround the building, the dogs being held back in case the suspect made a break for it. Once everyone was in position, Lock approached the old door and grasped the cold, rusty handle and gave it a gentle shove to no avail.

'POLICE!' he yelled. 'Open the door and come out with your hands on your head!' No response.

Lock gestured to one of the armed officers and motioned for the man to join him. Counting to three silently and signalling the count with his fingers, he pulled his foot back and booted the door with all his strength. The old wood cracked and splintered, shards flying all over the place and the door swung open.

Taking a deep breath, Lock entered, closely followed by his armed colleague and he couldn't believe the sight that greeted him. Michael Thompson and Sara Williams lay prone on the floor, side by side in a large pool of blood, a single knife discarded in the ground next to the girl. Dropping to his knees, he checked both their pulses – nothing. He couldn't believe it and sat, shocked, while his colleague radioed through for urgent medical assistance. Lock didn't say anything but he knew it was a worthless gesture, they were both already dead.

CHAPTER 46

Waking up, dazed and confused, Scott attempted to observe his surroundings through bleary eyes but it was his nose that gave him the answer of where he was. The unmistakable, overbearing scent of disinfectant burned the inside of his nostrils, mixed with the tinge of stale sweat. A waft of greasy, cheap food hung in the air and made his stomach churn – he was in hospital.

The heart monitor he was attached to was beeping away incessantly but as irritating as the sound was, at least it was an indication that he was still alive. An air conditioning system was gently humming away and he was grateful for the cool air that rushed over his warm, clammy body. Beyond the closed door of his room he could hear the distant chatter of hospital staff, patients and visitors alike, as well as the shrill ringing of multiple telephones.

Shifting uncomfortably in the hard, unforgiving hospital bed, he grasped the cold metal rail to pull himself into an upright position. The tiny movement was too strenuous for a man in his condition and it caused a searing pain to shoot up the side of his body. Gently clutching the area, he could feel the heavy bandaging beneath his hospital gown and the events that led to him being here came rushing back to him. Memories that unfolded in his mind and were just as painful as the knife that had punctured his flesh. The battle with the wanted man on the floor, thinking he had apprehended his foe and then the sudden hot pain caused by Sara plunging a blade into his body. All he had wanted to do was help her; years of sacrifice and unrelenting, obsessive searching to try and take her back to her life and she showed her gratitude by trying to kill him.

Rubbing wearily at his eyes, he managed to rid himself of the blurred vision and finally absorb his surroundings. The recognisable, pristine white of the hospital room stinging his sensitive eyes, the fluorescent lights causing the onset of an uncomfortable headache. There were a couple of empty seats and several bunches of flowers on a table on the far side of the room, their delightful scent obscured by the concoction of unpleasant hospital odours that dominated his sense of smell. To his right he had an empty cup and a large jug of water, pouring the liquid into the vessel he eagerly lapped at the cool liquid to try and quench the dryness in his mouth.

Returning the cup to its original position, he relaxed back into his pillows for a moment, allowing himself some time to try and digest what he had been through over the past few days. The realisation of what has unfolded was a tough one to swallow; Sara had stabbed him to help her captor getaway, an eventuality that Scott could have never foreseen. He had been left for dead, in the same room where her life had been stolen from her and they had escaped. He just hoped that his colleagues had made it there in time to capture Michael and rescue her, he didn't want all of his efforts to be in vain. He wasn't going to obsess over that now however, he knew all of his questions would be answered sooner rather than later.

Suddenly, the door to his room swung open and a nurse walked in, clearly shocked to see Scott wide awake and sat upright.

'Oh Mr Harris, it's so nice to see you awake.' She said pleasantly and followed the statement with a friendly smile. 'How are you feeling?'

Scott made to reply but instead emitted a raspy croak from his dry throat, grabbing the water he took a large gulp and tried again.

'G-good, I think.' He cleared his throat. 'I mean, I'm exhausted and very sore but it seems like I'm lucky to be alive so I'm not going to complain too much.' Scott attempted a smile but it came across as more of a grimace. The nurse recognised the intent and smiled back.

'Well that's good to hear Mr Harris.' she said as she flicked through some paperwork she had just retrieved from a holder from the end of his bed. 'I'm going to go and get the doctor and he can explain everything to you in more detail.'

Scott nodded and the nurse vacated the room, closing the door behind her. He waited patiently for the doctor to come to him with more information, hoping he wouldn't have to stay in here for too long – the odour was already doing his head in.

After several minutes, his door swung open once more and a tall man of Indian descent walked into his room, a large smile stretched across his handsome, slightly unshaven face. Clutching a clipboard and his stethoscope rested across the shoulders of his white lab coat, he approached Scott's bed.

'Mr Harris!' He yelled out jovially, in a thick, Indian accent. 'It's a pleasure to finally meet you properly! I am Doctor Saj Pavel, I was the one who performed your surgery.'

'Er… likewise.' Scott stuttered, a little startled by the energy of the man who stood at his bedside.

'So I suppose you want to know the extent of the damage?' Scott nodded, a silent response. 'Well, when you arrived here, you were not in good shape. Your

heart had stopped beating on the way here, the paramedics did a fantastic job to keep you alive! Once
you arrived, you had lost an awful lot of blood and
the damage from the wound seemed quite exten-
sive.' Doctor Pavel paused. 'We rushed you into the
operating theatre for surgery and a blood transfusion.
Luckily for you, the blade missed your vital organs
and we were able to repair the damage quickly. The
window of opportunity we had to save you was small
but we managed to get it done with time to spare!' The
final statement was said with uninhibited pride and
confidence, accompanied by a beaming smile from
the surgeon.

Scott sat silently, dumfounded, allowing the
onslaught of information to settle. He had *died?*
He had died and been brought back to life by these
incredible medical personnel. The realisation was
overwhelming and Scott sat unmoving, shocked at the
thought. Doctor Pavel waited patiently and allowed
Scott a few moments before speaking again.

'Now, everything looks fine and you will make
a full recovery but we would like to keep you in
for another twenty-four hours to monitor you. If
everything looks healthy after that, you'll be able to
go home.' Smiling again, the doctor turned to leave.
'I'll be back to check on you later.' With that, he left
the room.

Scott sat frozen, reeling from the information he had just been given. His heart stopping and being that close to death was a terrifying thought. Slumping back down in his bed, his head spinning, he began to drift off. A mixture of this new information and the trauma his body had suffered had left him shattered. His eyelids grew heavy and he didn't resist, closing his eyes he allowed himself to slip into a much needed slumber.

Several hours had passed when Scott finally arose from a deep, restful snooze, the unwelcome aromas of the hospital greeting him like a relative you wish you could avoid, giving him an immediate reminder of where he was. Opening his eyes, he yawned and stretched like a feline waking from a cat-nap. His attention was immediately drawn to a shape in his peripheral, one of the previously empty seats was now occupied by his friend and former colleague, James Lock.

Smiling, Lock greeted his old superior. 'Good to see you alive and well, Boss.'

Scott awkwardly and painfully shifted himself upright, groaning from the discomfort and looked at his friend.

'Did we get him, James?' Scott asked immediately, eager to finally know the outcome.

Lock didn't answer straight away, instead he fidgeted a little awkwardly in his seat, his eyes looking down at the floor. Even without looking at Scott, he could feel the former detective's stare burning into his soul. Eventually summoning the courage to answer, he looked up into Scott's eyes.

'Yes, we got him Scott... but not in the way you would hope.' Scott stared unblinking, a confused expression drawn across his tired face and Lock continued. 'After you called me, we got there as quickly as we could. I brought everyone, and I mean *everyone*, uniforms, dogs, the chopper, you name it. We arrived and there was a car chase which led to a serious collision between two of the patrol cars... one of our officers died at the scene. It was chaos and, from that chaos, Michael made off on foot with Sara.' He paused once more, hesitant to continue and Scott waited patiently. 'When we finally got to them, they had holed up in an old barn... and Sara had killed Michael... and then she took her own life. I'm so sorry mate.'

Scott was frozen, shocked and distraught, his heart began to race and his breathing became erratic and out of control, the beeping of his heart monitor picking up pace in tandem with his reaction. Tears followed, thick and fast, that poor girl! Brainwashed to believe that she had to end her own life, rather than live without her captor. Brainwashed to the point where she had stabbed the man that was trying to help her, the only person who hadn't given up on her. Scott's sobs were body-shuddering and painful but the loss of this young girl hurt more than any physical pain ever would.

Lock, unsure of how to approach his clearly devastated friend, attempted to reassure him and calm him down.

'I know it isn't the result we were after, mate but at least it's over. He can't hurt you or anyone else ever again.'

Scott looked up suddenly, realising that Lock was referring to his stabbing. They assumed it was Michael who had committed the act! In that moment he knew he would never reveal the truth, he would take that secret with him to the grave.

EPILOGUE

Standing outside the church, Scott gazed across the adjoining landscape. The air was crisp and refreshing, lucid sunshine beaming down from a cloudless blue sky, so bright it even made the old, moss-covered headstones look full of life. Small birds flittered in and out of a mature yew tree which swayed in the gentle breeze, its needles rustling in the wind. It was chilly out but Scott had protected himself against the cold with a long, black, wool overcoat which covered a smart black suit; black leather shoes and gloves completed the ensemble.

It was a beautiful Autumn day but, unfortunately, the weather did not match the mood. It had been ten days since that fateful night, the night that had almost killed him, the night when Sara and Michael had died, and he was at the church that day to attend Sara's funeral. The funeral of a girl he had grown attached to without ever having met her properly, a girl he had given up so much for and worked so hard to rescue but had ultimately failed.

Hoards of people were flooding past where he stood and he kept his back to them, avoiding the unwanted stares. The national press had ensured the conclusion of Sara's long-known disappearance was well covered and his name and face had been plastered across every newspaper in the country. He was being touted as a hero, a man of courage, all because he almost lost his life trying to get to her, but the labels were neither wanted nor welcomed. Absentmindedly, he gently caressed the area where he had been stabbed, the wound was a permanent reminder of that night but not a scar that needed to be celebrated or used as a reason to herald him as selfless. To him, he was just doing his job, doing what anyone in his position would have done and he didn't want the media giving him special treatment. They had even arrived at the funeral today, the vultures, carrying their cameras and snapping away and the bereaved – the behaviour disgusted him.

Although having never confirmed it, he had led everyone to believe that it was Michael who had stabbed him, not wanting the girl's memory to be tarnished. There had already been too many questions as to why she had taken her own life but they had put it down to not being able to cope with the fact that she had been forced to take someone's life. Only Scott knew the truth, knowing that she had stabbed him to protect her captor and by killing Michael, and taking her own life, had ensured they would never have to live apart – almost like a modern day Romeo and Juliet.

Finally turning around, he watched as the final few attendees ascended the stone steps to the church entrance and he moved to follow them, avoiding making eye-contact with any of the journalists or photographers who were yelling his name, and he suddenly felt a large hand on his shoulder. Spinning around he was met by the boyish face of James Lock.

'Alright mate.' It was a form of address, rather than a question as Lock greeted Scott amiably. The two men grasped each other in a firm embrace, 'How are you feeling?' Lock eventually enquired after they had let go of each other.

'Honestly? Bloody awful. The thought of going in there, seeing her coffin… it makes it all too… real.'

Lock nodded, a silent yet understanding response, he knew how hard his friend had been hit by the death of the young woman.

'I know what you mean, it already feels like that night was an eternity ago and I keep hoping it was all a nightmare… The multiple funerals bring me back to reality though.' He was referring to their colleague's funeral, only two days prior, the man who had lost his life in the collision during the car chase.

'You're not wrong there, mate' Scott responded and realised they were the only two left outside the church. 'Oops, we better head in.'

The two men hurriedly climbed the short, stone staircase in unison, neither of them looking back at the press, whose camera shutters were clicking away furiously. The large, heavy, wooden door of the church was open and as they approached they could hear the hushed tones of respectful chatter, a collective whisper that hauntingly drifted around the place of worship.

Entering the grand building, trying not to draw any attention to themselves, they took their seats in a vacant pew at the very back of the nave. Several heads turned to gawk at the detective and former detective who sat side by side, staring straight ahead and ignoring the stares. Scott glanced around, drinking in the sights in front of him; easily a couple hundred mourners had come, almost every seat in every pew was occupied. Sunlight streamed in through the large, stained-glass windows, casting colourful patterns throughout the room. Down the front, multiple candles had been lit and their flames danced in the gentle draft of air that wafted through the room but the bit that caught his eye was the coffin, the coffin that contained the lifeless body of the girl he had spent years trying to save.

Seeing the coffin for the first time brought a lump to his throat which he stifled, choking it down painfully.

Reality had crept up on him at that very moment, he never had been very good at processing his emotions and the sudden acceptance that her life was well and truly over was hitting him like a tonne of bricks.

As he stared at the coffin, he saw just how beautiful it was; made from pine and expertly varnished, it shimmered in the surrounding candlelight, the handles and details were a stunning bronze and the top was laden with colourful wreaths and flowers. It baffled him how something so eye-catching could be the symbol of so much sadness and grief. His stare was intense and he didn't drop his gaze, almost as if he was willing her back to life.

Snapping out of his daydream, his attention was grabbed by the vicar taking his place behind the lectern and a hushed silence fell across the room. 'Let us pray,' the vicar instructed, his voice echoing from the speakers that were positioned around the large space. Scott hung his head, along with the majority of the room as the vicar recited an old prayer before going on to talk about Sara. Scott blocked out the words, finding it all too difficult to listen to but his resolve was broken by the distraught, heartbroken cries of Janet Williams at the front of the room. Her sobs echoed around the large space, several others shedding tears as if they were contagious – empathy and grief was a powerfully emotive combination.

The service continued in the same vein, different verses being recited, interspersed with hymns and poems, and before long it was time for the final eulogy. Peter Williams, Sara's father, slowly, almost reluctantly took his place behind the lectern. Every set of eyes in the place were trained on him as he awkwardly prepared himself, every set of ears waiting and listening intently, so silent you could hear a pin drop. Peter looked tired and drawn, his sorrow obviously etched across his face and he took his time, allowing himself a few moments to get composed before beginning his reading.

'Today we mourn the loss and celebrate the life of our beautiful daughter.' He stopped to take a slow, deep breath before continuing. 'I wasn't certain I would be able to stand up here and do this but if Sara were here she would be telling me to stop being a wimp and get on with it.' He chuckled to himself and gentle laughter rippled across the room. 'It would be easy for me to stand here and obsess over the events which led to this day but I don't want her to be remembered for that. I want her to be remembered as the kind, caring, funny, beautiful young woman she was. Even as a child she was hilarious, I lost count of the amount of times we'd be about to leave the house and I'd be greeted with "Is that really what you're wearing, Daddy?" Obviously, I would change my clothes.'

More laughter drifted across the church hall. 'That behaviour continued right up through her teens but unfortunately my dress sense didn't get any better. She was always caring, always loving and thinking about others and as you can see by this amazing turnout, she was a popular girl. I'll never know how Janet and I managed to create someone so perfect, she was special, she was ours and this world, *our world,* won't be the same without her-' His voice trailed off to be replaced instantly with heart-wrenching cries of angst and he removed himself from the lectern.

Walking over to his daughter's coffin, he placed a hand on the side of it, his body shuddering from his sobs and said a few words which weren't decipherable from the back of the room. As he stood there, *U2's 'With or Without You'* began to play over the speakers and Peter was joined by five other men, all family members ready to carry the coffin through the church and back to the hearse. After a round of tender embraces, the six men hoisted the casket onto their shoulders and began the long walk out of the church, the entire room on their feet as a show of respect.

As the coffin passed where Scott stood with Lock, he suddenly came over all faint and wobbled, just about keeping himself upright by grabbing the back of the pew in front of him. The moment passed as quickly as it came but he knew that the outcome of this case would be something that would stay with him for the rest of his life.

● ● ●

Two days after Sara Williams had been laid to rest, Scott found himself outside a crematorium, about to attend another service. The unseasonably sunny weather had passed, to be replaced by a gloomier, wetter setting and a misty blanket of rain swept over him and the umbrella he clutched.

Approaching the entrance to the crematorium, his footsteps gently splashing in the pooling water, he glanced around at his surroundings. The car park was completely empty when he had arrived and that hadn't changed, there were no people outside and no signs that there would be anyone else turning up – the emptiness was eerie.

Reaching the door, he shook the moisture from his umbrella before folding it up and leaning it in the corner of the small entrance hall. Removing his rain-soaked jacket, he folded it over his arm and walked to the next door, the one that led to the main room. Pinned on the door was a sign that read 'IN MEMORY OF MICHAEL THOMPSON'. Nudging the door open, he walked into the main room and looked around; it was completely empty, not a single seat was taken and at the front there was a plain coffin, no flowers, no wreaths, no messages of love or grief.

Scott wasn't here to pay his respects or say good-bye, he was here because he needed proper closure, he wanted to ensure that this abhorrent human being was gone for good – just knowing he was dead wasn't enough. As he walked to the front of the room, the officiator appeared from a side-room; a short, plump, balding man with a friendly face and an awkward smile.

'Oh wonderful, we can start!' he exclaimed.

Scott was a little taken aback. 'Are you really not expecting any more people?' he asked.

'Well, seeing as the service was supposed to start half an hour ago, not really.' The man smiled his awkward smile. 'If you would be kind enough to take a seat, I can begin.'

Scott sat, as requested, and the officiator took his place and began to speak. The words were lost on Scott, who didn't pay any attention to the details, instead his eyes were focussed on the coffin that contained his nemesis. Rage built up from the pit of his stomach, a hot, fiery ball of anger which felt so intense he thought he was going to vomit. This disgusting individual had caused so many people unimaginable pain and suffering, and destroyed the life of an innocent girl.

After what felt like hours, the officator stopped talking and a large velvet curtain began to obscure the coffin, signifying the end of the service and Scott welcomed the gratification he needed so badly.

Once the coffin was completely hidden, he stood up, nodded curtly to the man and walked out of the crematorium. As he wrapped his jacket around his shoulders and opened his umbrella, he could feel himself smiling. For the first time in weeks, he was smiling. Strolling out into the gentle precipitation, he felt as though a huge weight had been lifted from his shoulders, a burden he had carried for so long was finally gone.

Reaching his car, he got in and pulled his phone from his jacket pocket, he'd had it on silent mode while he was in the crematorium, and he saw he had four missed calls from Lock. Calling his friend back immediately, it barely rang before an excitable Lock answered.

'Where have you been?' he yelled.

Scott was caught off guard by the sudden shouting but laughed it off.

'I had something to take care of, what's your problem?'

'You need to get down to the station, ASAP! Nick resigned yesterday and they want to make you Superintendent!'

Scott couldn't believe what he had just heard, he hadn't even expected to get his job back, let alone get a promotion. He was silent for a few moments, allowing the surprising news to sink in.

'Scott?' Lock checked he was still there.

Scott pushed the 'start' button on his car and the engine fired into life.

'OK, mate. I'll be there shortly.' With that, he hung up, placed the phone on the passenger seat and he was on his way.

ABOUT THE AUTHOR

Tom Franks is a former forestry worker turned crime fiction/ thriller writer.

He was born and raised in Hampshire, England but now resides with his American wife in Colorado, USA.

Tom is a keen rugby player and fan, lover of dogs and good whisky.

He excelled in literature at school and college, especially creative writing. At the age of 16, he wrote a short-story, for a GCSE coursework piece,that received top marks and was used as a 'perfect example' of creative writing for several years after.

15 years later, while navigating the American green card process, which didn't allow him to work, he had been given the gift of time. He used that time to turn that short-story into the prologue for his novel 'Little Lamb' and then built the story from there.

His aim with his writing is to create suspenseful thrillers that are so gripping, so captivating, it can give you a complete break from the stresses of everyday life.a smart black suit; black leather shoes and gloves completed the ensemble.

More Books From

PERFECT PUBLISHING

www.PerfectPublishing.com

Made in the USA
Monee, IL
01 April 2022